Eye of the Beholder

By

Marilyn Lee

This is a work of fiction. Names, characters, places, and incidents are products of the author's imagination or are used fictitiously and are not to be construed as real. Any resemblance to actual events, locales, organizations, or persons, living or dead, is entirely coincidental.

Eye of the Beholder by Marilyn Lee

Red Rose™ Publishing
Publishing with a touch of Class! ™
The symbol of the Red Rose and Red Rose is a trademark of Red Rose™ Publishing

Red Rose™ Publishing
Copyright© 2007 Marilyn Lee
ISBN: 978-1-60435-907-7
ISBN: 1-60435-907-2
Cover Artist: Shirley Burnett
Editor: Vi Bowen
Line Editor:

Red Rose™ Publishing
www.redrosepublishing.com
Forestport, NY 13338

Thank you for purchasing a book from Red Rose™Publishing where publishing comes with a touch of Class!

Chapter One

It was still dark outside when Carolyn Jordan woke. She could see through the pink and white curtains at the bedroom windows that Daddy always left slightly open. Yawning and blinking, she looked at the Big Bird alarm clock on the night stand next to her bed. Five-thirty. Clutching her stuffed Big Bird toy against her chest, she climbed out of bed and ran barefoot down the dimly lit hall.

The door to Daddy's room was open, but the room was dark. She climbed onto the padded chair Daddy kept under the light switch. She turned the knob until the room was bathed in the soft glow of the two rose-colored lamps on either side of the big bed where her daddy still slept.

Daddy hated getting up in the morning. But that was okay, because he had her to help him. Like Mommy used to do. Soon, maybe he'd have Diana to help him too.

She climbed out of the chair and skipped across the hardwood floor to the bed. It was big and reminded her of the sled she and Daddy used to go sliding down the hill behind the house when it was cold and icy. She had nice memories of cuddling in the bed between Mommy and Daddy when she was still scared of sleeping alone.

Now there was just Daddy—and her to take care of him. She climbed onto the bed and watched him. She liked watching him as he slept. Sometimes when he was awake, he seemed sad. Not when he was asleep.

Daddy had nice, dark brown hair. Granny said he should cut it, but Mommy always liked the way it curled on Daddy's forehead and neck when he was sleeping—and so did Carolyn.

She climbed onto Daddy's chest and kissed his cheek. She giggled as the hair on his face tickled her nose. "Daddy. Daddy, it's time to get up."

"Go away."

"Daddy! It's time to get up," she said, pushing against his shoulder.

He groaned and opened his eyes.

She wished her eyes were blue like his, but Daddy said her green eyes went perfectly with her blond hair—just like Mommy's.

"Morning, Daddy!"

"Tell me it's Saturday," he said.

"It's Friday and time to get up. You can sleep as late as you like tomorrow."

"Okay, you slave driver," he said, smiling. "So it's time to rise and shine?"

"And thank the Lord for another day," she reminded him. "You keep forgetting to say that."

Daddy looked away, and she bit her lip.

"Daddy?" She touched his cheek. "Are you thinking about Mommy again and feeling sad?"

Daddy hugged her and nuzzled his nose against her cheek. "I'm thinking how lucky I am to have you to remind me of the really important things, sweetie." He smiled. Daddy's smile always made her feel safe and warm. "Now, how about you go get washed, and we'll meet downstairs for breakfast when you're through? Can do?"

"Can do."

"That's my sweetheart."

She liked being Daddy's sweetheart. She grinned and jumped off the bed. Alone in the room, David sighed. This was the time of the day when he missed Harriet so much he might have lost her last week instead of sixteen months earlier. But lying there feeling sorry for himself wasn't going to change a thing.

He slipped out of bed and headed for the bathroom. After a quick shower, he dressed in his work clothes. Mornings in late April in Philadelphia could be downright frosty. He pulled on a long-sleeved thermal top, covered it with a flannel shirt, slipped on a pair of jeans, and stepped into safety boots before going downstairs to the kitchen.

Twenty minutes later, he and Carolyn were having breakfast. Harriet had loved this house and had spent literally months furnishing it. Every room in the house reminded him of her. But the kitchen with its white tiled floor, cherry wood cabinets and the big oval table he and Harriet had spent three weekends refinishing was most reminiscent of her.

"Daddy, do you like women?"

He blinked and refocused his gaze on the paper, playing for time. He knew pretending not to have heard the question wouldn't work, so he deliberately finished his coffee before looking up.

Carolyn's eyes were trained on his face as she awaited his answer, her milk forgotten.

"Yes. Your mother was a woman and you know I loved her." He glanced at his watch. "I think it's time we made a move." Folding his paper, he rose.

"Don't you want to know why I asked that question, Daddy?"

He knew why. Both Carolyn and his mother had been trying to get him to meet one of the owners of the daycare center where Carolyn spent her early mornings and late afternoons after her kindergarten class.

He'd met and interviewed Becki Howard, the other owner who greeted the children and parents in the morning. He had yet to meet Diana Stuart, who was there in the afternoons.

"I know why, sweetie," he said patiently. "But we really don't have time to talk about it now."

"But that's what you always say, Daddy," she complained.

He began stacking the breakfast dishes in the sink. "That's because it's always true," he said. "I know you miss your Mommy, and so do I, but I'm just not ready to start dating yet, sweetie."

"Well, when are you going to be ready, Daddy?"

"I'll let you know."

"But you would be ready if you met Diana, Daddy. She's so pretty and so nice. I know you'd like her as much as I do. And that's an awful lot."

"Since she's so pretty and nice, she's not going to be interested in meeting me. She must already have a man in her life."

"No she doesn't, Daddy. I told her about you and I think she wants to meet you."

"We'll see," he said. "Now come on, sweetie. Time to get a move on."

"Oh, all right, Daddy, but you don't know what you're missing."

He smiled. Like Harriet, Carolyn had to have the last word.

David spent a busy morning at the construction site where he was foreman. Just before twelve o'clock, he spotted his assistant foreman, Mike, standing on a scaffolding above him.

He cupped his hands around his mouth and bellowed. "Mike! Yo! Down here on the double."

Mike nodded. He waited just long enough to see Mike start down the ramp before he turned and walked off the site to where his Chevy Blazer was parked on the wide, unpaved road.

By the time he reached the Blazer, Mike was at his elbow. "What's up, Dave?"

"I have to pick Carolyn up and take her to the daycare today. Keep an eye on that Jones guy, will you? I'm not sure he's going to work out on the crane."

"He'd better work out. We can't afford to lose another guy."

"Tell me about it." He climbed into his Blazer. "I'll be back in about thirty or forty minutes."

He started the Blazer, put the engine in gear, and drove off. Carolyn's school was fifteen minutes away. He drove fast but carefully, glancing frequently at his dashboard clock. He didn't want to be late. Having lost Harriet, Carolyn was fearful of losing him too. He sighed with relief as the big, three-story school building came into view. He pulled into the parking lot and jumped out of the Blazer, just as Carolyn's kindergarten class recessed for the day.

"Daddy! Daddy!" Carolyn screamed in delight and ran across the school yard to him. The moment she reached him, she wrapped her arms around his legs and hugged him.

He lifted her into his arms and kissed her cheek. "Hello, sweetie."

Carolyn wrapped her arms around his neck. "Hi, Daddy. I didn't know you were coming for me this week. Where's Granny?"

"She has a doctor's appointment." He carried her to his Blazer. "So I'm taking you to the center."

"Oh, good. Then you can meet Diana, Daddy," Carolyn said happily as he fastened her into her safety seat in the rear of the Blazer. "She's nice and real pretty. Almost as pretty as Mommy was. I just know you'll like her."

He stifled a groan. With the new townhouse development running over budget and several guys out sick with the flu, his patience was tending to be on the non-existent side. He was not in the mood to socialize.

"Daddy, did you hear me?"

"Yes, honey, I heard you." He started the engine. "You were telling me how much I'll like your Diana."

And it was time they met. Carolyn was so fond of Diana Stuart, he needed to see for himself what type of person she was. Just so he knew Carolyn was in as good hands in the afternoons as she was in the mornings.

"Daddy, are you listening?"

"Yes," he said absently. "You were saying something about a parents' day at the daycare."

"It's the Friday after next. Are you going to come, Daddy?"

"Yes." It would be difficult to take any time off from work with the builders complaining about cost overruns, but he wasn't going to disappoint Carolyn. "I'm coming."

"Oh, good. I was afraid you wouldn't be able to come. Granny says you work too hard."

"I wouldn't miss it, honey," he assured her.

She settled into her seat and picked up her favorite book, *The Cat in the Hat.*

He turned onto a quiet, tree-lined street. He stopped his SUV in front of a big Victorian house with a big front lawn. He glanced at the bright yellow and white sign on the side of the building which bore smiling, childish faces. Happy Time Daycare.

"There it is, Daddy," Carolyn said.

"I know, sweetie," he said, smiling at her enthusiasm. "I have been here before." He got out of the Blazer, unbuckled Carolyn, and lifted her onto the sidewalk. Carolyn took his hand in hers and skipped happily along the driveway. "Come meet Diana, Daddy!"

"I'm coming, already, honey."

She squeezed his fingers. "Oh, Daddy! I'm so excited."

He gently returned the pressure of her small fingers before he stopped her and knelt at her feet. "Honey, I don't want you to get too excited. I told you that I'm not ready to start dating again yet. Remember?"

"But that's only because you haven't met Diana yet, Daddy. I just know you'll like her. Everybody does."

He sighed. It was hopeless. Like Harriet, once Carolyn got a hold of an idea, she didn't let go. "And I'm sure I will like her, but honey, liking her and wanting to date her are not the same thing. You understand that?"

She nodded impatiently, tugging at his hand. "Don't worry, Daddy." She stroked a hand down his cheek. "It'll be all right. You'll see. Okay?"

"Okay," he said, but he had a bad feeling. Carolyn was just too attached to Diana Stuart.

"Come on, Daddy." She tugged at his hand. He got to his feet and allowed her to lead him along the sidewalk toward the house.

The big, oak door opened just before they reached the house. A woman with a radiant smile and beautiful skin the color of a jar of dark, sweet honey stood there. She was full-figured and looked around five feet, ten inches. She wore her short dark hair in a mass of curls that provided a perfect frame for her pretty face. While the white coveralls she wore were far from flattering, they did tend to draw attention to her lovely, dark skin tone.

Was this the woman Carolyn and his mom thought he would be attracted to? Granted, she was pretty...very pretty, but—

"Diana! Look who I bought with me. My daddy!" Carolyn cried as if she'd just produced him out of a hat. "Isn't he cute?"

He was too used to Carolyn's outspokenness to be embarrassed. As, it seemed, was Diana Stuart, because she showed no signs of discomfort as she smiled warmly at Carolyn. "Hi, honey."

She had a slightly husky, sweet voice and a rather enchanting smile with full, lush-looking lips. Nice, but not nice enough to tempt him into dating again.

"Hi, Daddy," the woman said cheerfully, meeting his gaze head on and sticking her hand out. "Carolyn's been telling me how good-looking you were." Her dark brown eyes were warm as they lingered on his face. "I see she didn't exaggerate. I'm Diana Stuart."

His tentative smile vanished and he took a step backwards, startled by her frankness. But she was standing in front of him, her hand still extended. With Carolyn looking anxiously on, he responded in the only way he could. He moved closer to shake her hand. His nose twitched in appreciation as he caught a faint scent of her perfume; soft and feminine—like her hand in his.

"Hello, Daddy," she said again.

He shook her hand briefly. "I'm David Jordan, Mrs. Stuart,"

12

"Miss," she corrected, smiling. "I'm not married."

He kept his voice neutral. "So, I hear."

"Is that ice-cold tone meant to put me firmly in my place?"

That had been his intent, but it hardly seemed diplomatic to admit it. He arched a brow and shrugged. "That's not my place."

"Good. So, Daddy, any truth to the rumor that you're not seeing anyone either?"

He stared at her in amazement. Didn't the woman have any shame? "I wouldn't pay too much attention to rumors if I were you, Miss Stuart."

"But you're not me, are you, Daddy?"

"No." Maybe she thought it was cute to keep calling him Daddy, but it annoyed him.

"And you haven't answered my question."

"And I'm not going to, Miss Stuart."

"Okay. That was definitely a rebuke."

He glanced at his watch. "I have to get back to work."

She nodded silently.

He bent to kiss Carolyn. "See you tonight, sweetie."

"Didn't I tell you she was pretty, Daddy?" Carolyn demanded in a voice that Diana couldn't help but overhear. "Isn't her skin a pretty color, Daddy?"

He responded in the only way he could. "Yes," he said shortly and stood up.

He noted a hint of embarrassment in Diana Stuart's eyes, but she met his gaze head on. "Carolyn's a sweet child, Mr. Jordan."

She sounded sincere. Maybe even a little chastened. He nodded, softening toward her. "Thanks. Well, I have to go."

"Well, it was ... ah, ... nice to meet you."

Not judging by the coldness in her voice. "Ah...you too."

"Daddy's coming to parents' day, Diana," Carolyn piped in. "Isn't that great?"

"Oh, yeah. That's great, honey." She glanced up at him. The warmth was gone from her gaze this time and he knew she'd gotten his message. Just as he was beginning to wonder if maybe he hadn't been a bit hasty in sending it.

Because instead of being pleased that she was no longer flirting with him, he was aware of a wish to have that warm gaze of hers turned on him again while her dark eyes twinkled at him. He gave himself a mental shake. *Get a grip. She is not your type.*

"I have to go."

"Don't let us keep you, Mr. Jordan," she said in a flat voice. She took Carolyn's hand in hers. "Honey, say goodbye to your daddy."

"Goodbye, Daddy," Carolyn said obediently.

David nodded, gave Diana a quick glance, met her dark gaze, and reluctantly walked away.

Chapter Two

Diana made a circuit of the big playroom that took up a large portion of the first floor of the center. Then she moved onto the two other, smaller rooms. As she walked, she glanced down at the small figures of the children, napping on their bedrolls.

When she was satisfied that all the children were sleeping soundly, she made her way back to the big, old-fashioned roll-top desk at the back of the main room and slumped down into the comfortable, mahogany, leather chair.

She stared at the opposite wall, concentrating on the wallpaper. It had a white background with bluebirds sitting on pedestal fountains. It reminded her of the wallpaper in her room in the big, rambling Victorian house she'd grown up in on the other side of town.

She sighed. This would only happen to her. To finally meet a man she was attracted to only to find that he was as unfriendly as he was humorless. She again visualized his unsmiling face. What a Gloomy Gus. Imagine his mother and daughter thinking he was such a prize. She'd never seen anyone wear thirty years so hard.

Granted he was handsome, but he was definitely not someone of whom she wanted to see more. Since he still wore his wedding ring, he probably felt the same way. She grinned and shrugged. Not that she had to worry about that. Not after the way she'd practically come on to him. He obviously had not been impressed. Oh, well. Neither had she. *So get over it, girl.*

David couldn't get thoughts of Diana Stuart out of his head as he drove to his mother's house to pick Carolyn up after work. He didn't want to like her or think about her. Still, he found himself remembering the musical quality of her voice; the softness of her hand; the warmth of her gaze. She was undeniably attractive but also the most outrageous flirt he'd ever met.

Why had his mother thought he'd be attracted to someone so unlike Harriet? Harriet's shyness was one of the things he'd liked most about her. If it was one thing Diana Stuart was not, it was shy. So why was he even thinking of her?

He knew one thing about her for certain. She was a Christian. His mother would never have tried to interest him in a woman who wasn't deeply religious.

In which case, she's probably not interested in you. She was probably just in a flirting mood. He'd often noted pretty women liked to flirt. Although his parents had instilled a strong Christian faith in him, and he'd always tried to allow the Lord to guide his way, everything had changed with Harriet's death.

It was kind of hard to keep believing when a devout woman like Harriet was killed in a car accident, while the nineteen-year-old drunken driver walked away with just a few cuts and bruises. Where was the justice for Harriet, who had spent her days engaged in numerous church activities? Where was the fairness? Where was her reward for doing her best to be a good, decent Christian? He felt the familiar bitterness and rage forming a knot of tension and anger in his stomach. He took several deep breaths and released them gradually. Slowly, he relaxed his tense muscles.

Let it go, David. Think about something else. Feel something else. Anything else. He reached out and switched on the radio. The soft sounds of jazz filled the cab of the Blazer. He inhaled slowly and made the rest of the drive immersed in the music.

Ten minutes later, he turned into the back drive of the big, two-storied house where he'd been raised. The kitchen door opened before he reached it.

Carolyn came rushing at him. "Daddy! Daddy! You're here. Oh, Daddy, I missed you!"

He laughed and swung her up into his arms, kissing and hugging her. "I missed you too."

"Hello, dear."

He looked up to see his mother standing in the kitchen doorway. He smiled. At fifty-six, with dark hair cut close to her face, Gloria Jordan was still a petite, attractive woman. He kept expecting some eligible bachelor at her church to realize what a find she was and marry her.

"Hi, Mom." Shifting Carolyn to his other side, he bent to kiss his mother's cheek. "You look great."

She smiled and stepped out of the doorway. "How sweet, dear."

He followed her into the kitchen, set Carolyn on her feet, and took a slow, deep breath. His mom's kitchen always seemed appetizing. He walked over to the sink to wash his hands and then he headed for the refrigerator. He'd done his best to learn how to prepare meals over the last sixteen months, but so far he hadn't made much headway. Carolyn was a real trooper and always pretended to enjoy his efforts, but they left him longing for a real home cooked meal.

On the top shelf of the refrigerator, he spotted a small bowl of potato salad. Harriet had been an excellent cook, but nobody made potato salad like his mom made.

He reached in to retrieve the treasure, got a fork out of the drawer and sat back at the big wooden table where his father used to administer his father-to-son lectures. "You don't mind, do you, Mom?" he asked, almost as an afterthought.

"Of course not, dear," his mother said, smiling as she sat opposite him. "I'm glad you still enjoy my cooking."

"What's not to enjoy?" He lifted a forkful of salad to his mouth and closed his eyes as he began chewing. "Hmm. Mom, this is fantastic as always."

"Daddy!"

He paused and looked at Carolyn, who was sitting on a chair across from him. She stared at him with a look of disapproval of her pretty face.

"What? What's wrong, honey?"

"You didn't say grace!"

He had developed the bad habit of skipping grace when he was alone. "You're right." Bowing his head, he said a brief blessing, then dug into the salad again.

His mother gave Carolyn a glass of strawberry milk, then sat back at the table. "How was your day, dear?"

He swallowed a mouthful of salad. "All right. What about you, Mom? How did your doctor's appointment go?"

"Good." She smiled at him. "My pressure's under control and everything else is fine." She paused and he suspected she was searching for a way to broach the subject of Diana Stuart.

He finished the last mouthful of salad and waited.

"I understand you met Diana Stuart today."

He nodded.

"So what did you think of her, dear?" she asked.

He gave her a weary look. In the last four months, she had worn him down to the extent that he had allowed her to fix him up with two different women. She had assured him each was an "excellent prospect." However, neither had roused any sense of excitement in him nor made him want to get to know them. But Mom, being Mom, kept trying.

He shrugged. "She seemed nice enough."

"But? Go on," she urged. "What fault did you find with her?"

"That's it. No buts," he said, hoping that she'd let it go at that. "I didn't find any fault with her." He got up and took the bowl to the sink.

"Oh, leave that, dear."

"Thanks, Mom." He put the bowl in the dishpan, relieved not to have to wash it. At home he and Carolyn made a game of washing dishes, but if not for his mother's insistence that he had to raise Carolyn properly, he would have been content to eat with plastic utensils off paper plates.

He turned to look across the kitchen at Carolyn. "Ready to go sweetie?"

She finished her milk, nodded, and lifted her arms.

He scooped her up, kissing her on both cheeks. "We're going to head home now, Mom."

"Daddy didn't like Diana, Granny," Carolyn said, wrapping her arms around his neck.

"I didn't say that." Recalling how thoughts of her had lingered, he went on quickly. "I'm sure she's very...ah...very..."

"Nice, so you said," his mother replied, following them to the kitchen door. "But you're not interested in her?"

He turned with his hand on the back doorknob. "It's not personal, Mom. I'm not interested in any woman just at the moment."

"We're not talking about any woman. We're talking about a specific woman, David. We're talking about Diana Stuart. She's a good, kind, pretty woman any man would be glad to know."

He remembered her beautiful smile and warm gaze. "I'm sure she's all those things and more, but I'm just not ready to get involved with another woman yet."

"David, darling, I know these last months have been awful for you, but life has to go on for you and for Carolyn. You both need a woman in your life."

"I don't want another woman in my life, Mom." He glanced at Carolyn, who stared anxiously at him. Part of him knew his mother was right. Even if he didn't need or want another woman trying to take Harriet's place, he had to consider Carolyn. It was his next wife and Carolyn's step-mom that should be rousing him in the morning, not Carolyn.

The pain of losing Harriet was still too fresh. He couldn't bear the thought of filling her place in his heart with another woman.

"You need a woman in your life," his mother insisted, almost as if she'd read his mind. "You both do."

He leaned down and kissed her cheek. "Maybe so, but I can't handle it yet."

"But David, darling, you're doing yourself such a disservice. If I didn't think Diana was just right for you, I wouldn't push it. But I know she is. She's a—"

"Please, Mom! I know that's how you feel, but I don't agree. Can we please leave this discussion for another time?"

She nodded grudgingly. But he knew by the determined jut of her chin that he hadn't heard the last of how right for him Diana Stuart was.

"If that's the way you want it, dear."

Chapter Three

Daddy was quiet on the drive home from Granny's house, leaving all the talking to her. Carolyn didn't mind. Maybe Daddy was thinking of Diana. Maybe he'd decide he liked her after all. He just needed to see her again. Once he did, Carolyn was sure he'd see that Diana would make a perfect mommy for her and wife for him.

Only she didn't think Daddy would ask Diana out. Tomorrow was Saturday. She grinned suddenly. "Daddy, can we go to the park tomorrow?"

"Sure can, sweetie." Daddy smiled at her in his rearview mirror. "I drove past Tacony Creek Park tonight on the way to Granny's house. They have the new swing sets up."

"Oh, I don't want to go there, Daddy. I meant Wissahickon Park. Can we go there instead?"

"Wissahickon Park? Why? Tacony Creek is much closer and all the equipment is newer."

"It is?" For a moment, she was tempted to agree to go to Tacony Creek Park, but it was more important that she and Daddy went to Wissahickon Park. "It's closer to home so we can go there anytime. Let's go to Wissahickon Park tomorrow, Daddy. Please? Can do?"

"Can do, sweetie."

Carolyn smiled. "Thanks, Daddy."

"So he's a real hunk, huh? Did you check out those gorgeous blue eyes and that square chin? I told you you'd like him."

Diana and Becki were sitting in Diana's third floor apartment above the daycare center. The last child had been picked up half an hour earlier, and as usual, they were ending the work week with a well-deserved cup of green tea before Becki headed home.

Diana took several sips from her cup. "Good looking? No. He's not good looking."

Becki set her cup on the large white kitchen table. "You don't think he lived up to his billing?"

Diana shrugged. "Oh, okay. So he's sort of good looking. But only if you happen to like your men big, humorless, and as unfriendly as the day it long."

Becki studied Diana's face. "Unfriendly? He always seemed friendly enough when he dropped Carolyn off in the morning."

"Maybe to you, but he blew me off big time."

"Why?"

She bit her lip and shrugged. "Okay, maybe it was partly my fault. I sort of flirted with him."

Becki's arched eyebrows rose and her mouth formed a silent o. "You? You flirted with a man? You, Diana Stuart? The same Diana Stuart who's always telling me a woman has to be ladylike? That Diana Stuart?"

"I know who I am," Diana said, frowning. "And you don't have to rub salt in my wound, do you?"

"Oh, come on! You're pulling my leg."

"No, really. I wish I were," she said shaking her head in amazement at the memory. "You would have been embarrassed for me."

"How? Why?" She glanced up toward the ceiling as if seeking divine inspiration. "Why am I never here to see these things?"

"I'm glad you weren't here. It was awful. I don't know what came over me," Diana said in frustration. "The moment I saw him coming down the path, I just felt really...well, like my prayers had finally been answered. Still, I was okay and pretty cool until I looked into his eyes. He has the bluest eyes I've ever seen. I looked in his eyes, and the next thing I knew, I was flirting with him."

"You know, there's flirting, and then there's flirting. Maybe you weren't really flirting with him."

Diana centered her gaze on the white, vinyl wall behind Becki's head which bore a beautiful watercolor of a dozen red roses. "Oh, I flirted all right. I did everything but ask him for a date."

Becki snapped her fingers. "That's where you went wrong."

"Where? What should I have done?"

Becki arched her brows. "Went ahead and asked him for a date. What else?"

"Becki! Don't you get it? I should have stuck to hello, nice to meet you, and goodbye."

"Why?"

"Why? Good looking he may be, but he's not exactly the answer to my prayers." She saw the look on Becki's face and frowned. "Oh, I know you don't think much of waiting on God, but—"

"I didn't say that," Becki said quickly. "Did I say that? I don't think so. I don't know where you get your ideas, Diana. I believe in God as much as the next person. I just think there are some matters you have to take into your own hands. Finding a husband is one of them. But go on. Do you think the Lord wants you to wait until he sends you a black man?"

Diana shrugged. "I'm not usually into white guys, but he's so hunky and...those eyes..."

Becki smiled. "They're nice enough, Diana, but nothing to go on and on about."

She shrugged. "It doesn't matter because he definitely was not interested."

"Why not? You're pretty, super nice, you have a great sense of humor, and you can cook. What more could he or any other man want in a woman?"

"How about a little modesty?" Diana suggest. "I got the feeling I'd shocked him."

"You're plenty modest."

Diana shook her head. "You'll never get him to believe that. You should have seen the look on his face. He was embarrassed."

"The look on his face? Maybe you misread it. Maybe it wasn't embarrassment. Maybe it was…"

"What?"

"Oh, I don't know. I didn't see it. Are you sure he's not interested?"

"Trust me on that score. I think…" she hesitated, biting her lip. "He's probably one of those big men who prefer small women rather than plus-sized ones." She held her arms wide and glanced down at herself. Her father, born and raised in Georgia, had lovingly called her a down-home-healthy Georgia peach. Now, twenty-seven and still single, she'd learned that not all men went in for "healthy" women. "As you know, I'm not exactly small."

Becki frowned. "So? If he's too dense to appreciate all your virtues, it's his lost."

Diana smiled. Becki had been a loyal friend since they'd met in their junior year in college. "That's one way of looking at it," she said.

"That's the only way. If he's too much of a jerk to realize when he's struck gold, it's his loss."

Diana laughed. "Let's not get carried away, Becki. I wouldn't exactly call meeting me striking gold."

"No? Well, on the off chance that you're right about this guy, maybe it's time to rethink your game plan. I know you only want to meet a nice, Sunday-go-to-meeting type guy, but there are some very nice, available guys that aren't heavy into religion. Why don't you give one of them a try?"

Not that again. She held up a hand to stop Becki. "Because I need to share everything with the man I marry. My joys, my sorrows, my hopes, my dreams. Most especially, my faith."

"How do you know that won't come in time? Maybe you can change him. You know, help him see the light, as it were."

She shook her head. "Sometimes it's all I can do to keep myself together. Anyway, I couldn't marry a man who didn't have a close relationship with God."

"Why not?" Becki demanded, sounding annoyed.

"Because my faith is very important to me. I want to spend my life with a man that will help reaffirm it, not challenge it. Or worse, try to subvert it."

Becki shrugged, finished her tea, and got to her feet. "Suit yourself, Di. But you're letting a lot of nice guys needlessly slip right through your fingers. But hey, it's your fingers and your life."

"Yes, it is," she agreed. "And that's how I choose to live it."

"Fine, but if you change your mind, I know a couple of guys who would love to meet you." Becki winked. "And some of them like women with a little meat on their bones."

"Becki—"

"Hold your horses. They might not sing in the choir, go around singing the Lord's praises, but I don't think you have to do all those things to believe in God."

Which left Diana wondering exactly how these men's faith was manifested in their lives. After all, hadn't Jesus said you shouldn't hide your light under a bushel?

"Becki, I really appreciate your interest, but I can be patient until the right man comes along." *If he comes along,* an inner voice added. She tried to ignore it, but she was beginning to wonder how long she'd have to wait to meet her Mr. Right.

The next morning, after finishing her house work, Diana prepared for her Saturday morning walk. She donned a pair of sweats, put her wallet and house keys in a fanny pack, slipped an inspirational tape into her portable tape player, and left the apartment. She headed to Wissahickon Park, four blocks away.

She started off slowly, with short steps, barely moving her arms for the first two blocks. By the end of the fourth block, her steps had lengthened and she was swinging her arms briskly. She swung into the park and headed down the first of several curving, tree and grass lined pathways. As she walked, she smiled, enjoying the warmth of the afternoon sun on her face and the smell of fresh cut grass. Being in the park always filled her with appreciation for all that God provided.

She passed numerous people coming in the opposite direction, some walking, some jogging. To her right and left, people picnicked in the grass. She smiled at the families while quickly looking away from the couples. Giving them too much attention could lead to her coveting their happiness.

You'll get yours in time, Diana. You just need to hang on a little longer. The man of your dreams could be around the next bend, so don't lose hope. She took the last curve with renewed energy.

"Diana! Here we are! Over here, Diana!"

She glanced to her right in surprise. Carolyn Jordan sprang up from a blanket on the grass and came running towards her.

Diana came to a halt. Her gaze moved pass Carolyn. David Jordan sat with his back against a huge tree, staring at her in surprise.

By then Carolyn had wrapped her arms around Diana's legs. "What took you so long? Daddy and me have been waiting and waiting for you forever! I was beginning to think you weren't coming."

Over Carolyn's head, Diana saw David Jordan's blue eyes narrow and his lips press into a firm, disapproving line.

She suppressed a sigh. *Yeah, well, I'm real happy to see you too, Gus.*

"Diana?"

She smiled down at Carolyn. "This is a nice surprise, sweetie. I thought you said you went to Tacony Park? What are you doing here?"

"I knew you'd be here today, so me and Daddy came to see you. Aren't you surprised and glad we did?"

"I'm surprised all right," she said. She wouldn't have expected Carolyn's father to seek her out. She turned her attention to him.

He rose. Like her, he wore sweats and running shoes. "That's not exactly what happened, Miss Stuart," he said quickly. "Carolyn obviously knew you'd be here, but I didn't."

I want that understood. He didn't actually say the words, but he projected them at her. She felt them like a blast.

Their gaze met and locked briefly.

She saw nothing in his gaze to hint that he was glad to see her. Fine. He didn't like her. She smiled down at Carolyn before gently disengaging herself. "Seeing you here is a really nice surprise, honey, but I have to go."

"Oh, no, Diana. Me and Daddy brought lots of food. Please stay and share it with us."

"That's very generous of you, honey." She cupped Carolyn's soft cheek with her palm. "But I'll see you on Monday."

"Oh, but me and Daddy want you to stay!" Carolyn clutched her hand. "You can't go. We've been waiting for you forever."

Diana smiled down at her. She didn't look at David Jordan again, although she was aware of him standing less than two feet away from her. She could feel his gaze on her. "That's very sweet, honey, but I think your Daddy would rather I left. He didn't expect to run into me here today, and I'm sure he's looking forward to having you all to himself."

"He can have me to himself some other time, and I know he's glad to see you again." Carolyn turned to face her father. "Tell her, Daddy. Please tell her we both want her to stay."

When several moments passed without a response from him, Diana cast an amused look in his direction. He looked as implacable as the big tree he'd been sitting under. "You can relax now, Mr. Jordan. I'm leaving." She started back down the path.

"Daddy! She's going!" Carolyn's voice was raised in appeal to her father. "Why don't you say something? What are you waiting for?"

She'd only taken a few brisk strides when David Jordan called out to her in a reluctant voice. "Miss Stuart. Please. Wait."

She stopped, took a deep breath, and turned to face him. "It's all right, Mr. Jordan. Carolyn doesn't understand how it is, but I do."

To her surprise, he shook his head. "Actually, Miss Stuart, I don't think you do."

"I'm sure I do."

"We...Carolyn and I, would like you to stay."

"Wow. That must have hurt," she said.

He extended a hand towards her. "Please."

She should go. Everything in David Jordan's attitude affirmed his lack of interest in her. Why stay and make them both uncomfortable? But the irrational part of her that was attracted to him urged her to stay. She shook her head.

"We'd like you to stay, Miss Stuart."

She met his gaze and wavered. "I...well, if you're sure I'm not unwelcome."

"I'm very sure you're not unwelcome."

His firm assurance surprised. "You are?"

"I just said so, didn't I?" He moved his hand in a sweeping movement toward the blankets spread out on the grass under the big tree. "Forgive my manners. Carolyn and I would like you to join us."

His voice was pleasant, but impersonal.

That's probably as good as it was going to get, girl. She smiled. "I'd like to join you."

"Then do."

"Thank you." She sank down onto the blanket. Her heart pounded.

"I like this," Carolyn said, smiling hugely. "We're like a family. A daddy, a mommy, and a pretty daughter. Me."

Diana turned to find David Jordan staring at her. She lost herself in his blue gaze, unable to look away from him. Not really wanting to.

"Daddy's very good looking. Isn't he Diana?" Carolyn demanded in a satisfied voice.

Diana blushed and fought back the urge to agree with Carolyn. Finally, she dragged her gaze away from David Jordan's. She looked at Carolyn. "Ah, what...what do you have to eat?" She managed to keep her voice level.

"Lots of stuff," Carolyn began. "But you didn't answer my question about Daddy."

"And she's not going to," David said firmly.

"Why not, Daddy?"

"Instead of asking questions that are difficult for her to answer honestly, sweetcakes, why don't you tell Miss—"

"Oh, Daddy! Why do you keep calling her Miss like that? Her name's Diana."

He looked at Diana. "Carolyn seems to think I should call you Diana."

"Well, it is my name," she said airily.

"And mine's David."

"David is a nice name."

"Daddy's nice too," piped in Carolyn. "Nice and good looking."

Diana bit back the urge to disagree with the child. Nice was not the first word that came to mind when she thought of David Jordan. Good looking? Absolutely? Nice? Not so much.

"Daddy would make a really good husband," Carolyn confided, smiling at her.

"Oh?"

"Oh, yeah," Carolyn assured her. "Why don't you marry him?"

David looked absolutely horrified.

Diana's lips twitched. He must be afraid she'd take Carolyn seriously. She grinned. "No need to panic, Mr. Jordan." She laughed. "I almost never accept proposals from the young daughters of unwilling men on first dates."

His shoulders relaxed and he released a long breath. "That's a relief, but this is not a date, Miss Stuart."

"Diana, Daddy. Diana."

"Diana," he repeated, leaning back against the tree trunk.

The sunlight filtered down through the branches of the tree, streaking through his thick brown hair, sprinkling it with streaks of gold. She looked away. Life could be so unfair. There he was, hurting, lonely, and in need of a wife for himself and a mother for Carolyn. Here she was, willing and ready to be both, but held back by her size, his lack of interest, and possibly her skin color.

"Not to worry," she said again. "Despite what you might think, I'm not desperate for a man."

He straightened against the tree, his eyes widening. "Why would you think I thought that?"

"Don't you?"

"No! I'm very sure you have your share of admirers." He sounded sincere.

She hadn't been defensive about her size in a long time. She grinned suddenly. "Oh, yeah. I have so many of them they constantly trip over each other."

He nodded, still sounding and looking sincere. "I told Carolyn as much."

"Really? Are you in the habit of discussing my personal life with her?"

He gave her a wary look. "No, I am not."

"But?"

"But you must know that she and my mother would like us to...ah..."

She knew Carolyn had impossible dreams of her father falling for her the moment they met. The news that his mother shared that dream came as a revelation. "They want us to become a couple?"

"Ah...yes."

Her heart thumped. "And you would like?"

"Daddy would like it too, only he doesn't know it yet," Carolyn interrupted. "Will you wait for him until he does?"

Before she could answer, David groaned and spread a hand over his face. "This is going to be a long day."

Diana chuckled and reached into the picnic hamper for a sandwich. "Oh, I don't know about that. I'm not such bad company once you get to know me. Tell you what, let's make a deal."

He arched a brow and peeked at her through his splayed fingers.

She suppressed the urge to giggle like a teenager crushing.

"What kind of deal?" He sounded wary.

"Oh, nothing too earth shattering. Let's just agree to enjoy the day and let Carolyn speak her mind without either of us getting embarrassed."

He dropped his hand and cast a quick glance at Carolyn before looking at her again. "Oh, I don't know if that's such a good idea. Given enough encouragement, she'd have us engaged before the day's over."

She took a small bite of her sandwich; ham and cheese with too much mayo. She swallowed slowly and met his probing gaze. "And that would definitely be a bad thing."

His answer surprised her. "I didn't say that."

She swallowed slowly. "Oh?"

He shook his head. "But it's not going to happen."

That was his way of warning her off. Well, she already knew he wasn't interested. "Oh, lighten, up, Gu..." she bit her lip and swallowed a giggle.

He stared at her. "What were you about to call me?"

"Gloomy Gus." She shrugged. "Sorry. Slip of the tongue, but really, you're quite safe with me. I promise not to hold you to anything your delightful daughter says."

He grinned suddenly.

She sucked in her breath. His smile transformed his face. Instead of Gloomy Gus, he was now Dashing David.

"Deal," he said.

She flashed him a slow smile. "Unless of course, I get it in writing," she went on. "Then all bets are off."

His smile vanished.

She laughed and raised her brows to indicate she wasn't serious. "Oh, Gus."

After a moment, he laughed too.

"That's better. I was beginning to think you never smiled or laughed and it's too glorious a day not to do both."

He shrugged, sobering. "I haven't had a lot to be happy about lately, even on glorious days."

"I know," she said, softly. "But things can, and do change for the better."

"Do they?"

"Oh, yes. You just have to believe."

Carolyn slipped her arm through her father's. "Isn't this nice, Daddy?"

"Yes," he said slowly, sounding surprised. "It is."

Carolyn gave her a smug smile. "See Diana, Daddy's starting to like you already."

Diana shot David a wry look. "La de da," she said dryly and laughed.

David laughed too.

Although Carolyn clearly didn't understand, she laughed too.

After they'd eaten, David suggested they pack up and go bike riding. "There are several scenic bike trails nearby. We can rent bikes and check them out."

That's your hint that you've overstayed your welcome, and now it's time for you to get lost, girl. "Sounds like something Carolyn will love." She rose. "Well, thanks for the use of the blanket and the food."

He looked up at her. "You're leaving?"

"Yes."

He stood up. "You've misunderstood. I thought you might like to come with us."

She blinked at him. "Oh? Aren't you afraid we'll wind up married if we spend any more time together, today?" she teased.

"No." He shook his head. "Why should I when I have no intentions of putting anything binding in writing?"

So he did know how to lighten up. She feigned a sigh. "Just when I thought I was about to get to first base with you."

He laughed. "So, will you join us?"

He had a nice smile and a nicer laugh. She nodded. "Since you ask so nicely, yes, I will."

He smiled at her.

A delicious warmth spread slowly through her. Ignoring it, she turned to smile down at Carolyn. "What about you? Do you want me to go bike riding with you and your dear old dad?"

"You bet I do!" Carolyn said happily.

She turned to smile at David. "Seems like I'm all yours."

He stared down into her eyes.

She moistened her lips. "For the rest of the afternoon, that is."

"Only that long?" He shrugged.

Holy Hanna. He was flirting with her. She nodded.

He shrugged. "Oh, well, we'll have to make do with that, then."

"Careful," she warned.

"Of what?"

She leaned closer and lowered her voice. "If you flirt with me directly, I might take you seriously. Even if it's not in writing."

His only response was a slow, warm smile that set her heart knocking against her ribs.

Oh, Hanna! Things are getting interesting, girl. Just be careful and do not overplay your hand.

Chapter Four

That night, lying in bed, unable to sleep, David wished he could undo that afternoon at the park. He was at a loss to explain what had happened. One moment, he'd been angry because Carolyn had tricked him into going to the park to meet Diana. And nothing was going to convince him to ask Diana to join them. The next moment, he'd been sitting opposite her on the blanket, wondering how any woman could look so good in such unbecoming attire.

At the time he'd told himself he was asking her to stay strictly to please Carolyn. But he needn't have spent all afternoon enjoying her company just to please Carolyn. He hadn't asked her to go bike riding with them just to please Carolyn. And he sure wasn't thinking about her now to please Carolyn. Lying there thinking of her was a purely selfish indulgence. She was pretty, funny, and had the most delectable looking skin he'd ever seen. Thoughts of her smooth, dark skin made his hands ache to caress her.

Oh, David. Get a grip.

He knew that he'd need to think about remarriage soon. Carolyn wanted and needed a stepmother, and judging by the way he'd sat staring at Diana all afternoon, he needed a wife. But not Diana Stuart. Granted, her charming smile and warm personality made it difficult not to like her. In addition to being pretty, she was good for and to Carolyn who clearly adored her.

Having met her, he understood why his mother and Carolyn were so fond of her. But she was so completely different from Harriet that he couldn't seriously consider her anything but a friend. When he met a woman similar to Harriet in temperament, he'd ask her out. Until then, he would go on raising Carolyn the best he could.

He settled against the pillow and decided he wouldn't see Diana again. If he did, she might misunderstand his intentions. He wouldn't like to mislead or hurt her. She was too nice for that. She deserved the attention of a man prepared to adore her just as she was. Since he wasn't that man, he'd stay out of her way.

As he was falling asleep, he remembered parents' day at the daycare. He'd see her then. But that would absolutely be the last time. Of course, he'd see her when he dropped Carolyn off in the mornings at the daycare, but that was different. He wouldn't need to linger or even to really talk to her. He could be in and out within moments before she had time to flirt with him, or worse, make him want to flirt with her.

43

Diana woke before her alarm clock went off on Sunday morning. Cradling the extra pillow against her chest, she lay in bed, her mind filled with thoughts of David and Carolyn. She had enjoyed her day with them. Once he'd unwound, she'd found David could be as charming as he was handsome. Riding along the shady trails, the three of them had laughed and sung silly songs.

She'd found his gaze turned on her often enough to make it clear that he found her attractive. Despite herself, she'd begun to hope that maybe he liked her. That certainty had waned once their outing was over. He hadn't been very friendly when he'd driven her home, just before seven.

Standing at her door with him, she could find no traces of the charming man who'd spent most of the day flirting with her.

"Well, I'll see you around, Diana."

She studied his unsmiling face by the street light. Definitely Gloomy Gus. "Where?"

"Where what?"

"Where will you see me around?"

He shrugged. "When I drop Carolyn off here in the mornings."

And if that wasn't a brush off, she'd never had one. "Fine. I'll see you then." She waved at Carolyn, seated in the back of his vehicle, and hurried inside, afraid he'd see her disappointment reflected in her eyes.

Inside, she leaned against the closed door. She'd been foolish to think that one afternoon spent in her company would impress him so much that he'd want to get to know her.

Diana spent Sunday morning in church. The sermon on the need to be thankful for what the Lord provided was just what she needed. It felt like a personal message direct to her from the Lord.

While it was true she longed for a husband and children of her own, she had to face the possibility that it might not be the Lord's will for her. If that were so, she still had a lot for which to be thankful. She had a job she loved that provided an adequate income for her needs, she had many good friends, and she had her faith.

If it were the Lord's will for her to pass through life without the comfort and love of a husband and children, so be it. He had never let her down or asked too much of her. He had always provided for her needs. Not her wants, maybe, but surely for her needs.

David had Carolyn ready for Sunday morning services when his mother arrived to pick her up. He saw the quick compression of her lips when she noted he wore jeans and a pullover. She held her cheek up for his kiss. "David, it's only eight o'clock. Why don't you run upstairs and change so you can join us for services this morning?"

"Yeah, Daddy, why don't you come with us today?" Carolyn asked. "You haven't been to church for a really long time."

He shook his head. "Maybe next week. I have a lot to do around the house today."

His mother sighed and caressed his cheek. "Well, Carolyn and I had better get started then."

He walked them to the car, kissed both their cheeks, and saw them off.

He stood in the road, watching his mother drive off. He frowned. Harriet had worked very hard to instill a strong faith in Carolyn. How long would Carolyn's faith survive if he didn't appear to believe anymore? Harriet wouldn't have wanted that; neither did he. Maybe it was time he thought about going back to services for Carolyn's sake.

"Are you still mad at me, Daddy?"

David sat on the side of Carolyn's bed on Sunday night. He tucked her favorite yellow sheet under her chin before he kissed her cheek. "Still? Honey, I was never mad at you. Why did you think I was?"

"Because you've been very quiet all day and last night. I thought you were mad about the park and Diana. But you shouldn't be because you stared and stared at her like you liked her."

David chose his words carefully. "I'm not mad at you, Carolyn, but I do want you to understand that you and I have to be truthful with each other."

"But, Daddy, I didn't lie to you!"

"I know you didn't, sweetie." He touched her cheek. "Why didn't you tell me why you wanted to go to Wissahickon Park?"

She frowned. "I wanted to tell you, Daddy, but I didn't think you'd take me if I did. But I didn't lie to you, Daddy! Honest I didn't."

"No, but you did deliberately not tell me."

She stared up at him. "I know, but that's not the same as a lie. Is it?"

"Sometimes it can be very close to a lie."

She bit her lip. "Are you disappointed in me, Daddy?"

He shook his head. "No, but we have to be honest with each other. No more not telling me things you know I don't know. Okay?"

"Okay, Daddy. Can I ask you an honest question?"

"You can ask me anything, sweetie."

"Why don't you like Diana?"

"I never said I didn't like her, sweetie."

"But you don't. I thought you liked her at the park, but now I think you don't. Do you?"

David wasn't sure how to answer her question in a way Carolyn would understand. "You really like ice cream. Don't you, sweetie?"

She nodded, her eyes steady on his face.

"Vanilla is okay, but you love strawberry better than any other flavor."

She nodded again.

"Well, that's how I feel about Diana and women like your mom."

"I don't understand, Daddy."

"Well, your Mom was like strawberry ice cream. Diana's like vanilla ice cream. She's okay, but I prefer strawberry ice cream, or women who are like your mommy was. Do you understand what I'm saying?"

She shot up in bed, her eyes wide. "But Diana's not like ice cream! She's so nice and..."

He pressed a gentle finger against her lips to silence her. "But do you understand?"

She nodded with obvious reluctance. "Yes, Daddy, but —"

"That doesn't mean I don't like Diana or don't think she's nice or even pretty."

"You're not going to ask her out. Are you?"

He gently pushed her back into a reclining position. "No, Carolyn, I'm not."

"But, Daddy! She made you smile and laugh. I like her and I want you to go out with her."

"I know you do, sweetie, but we both have to like the woman I go out with." He bent to kiss her cheek. "Trust me?"

She threw her arms around his neck. "Yes, Daddy," she said sadly. "But I wish you'd change your mind about Diana."

"Sweet dreams, sweetie."

On Monday morning, when David walked into the center with Carolyn, Diana stayed in her seat at the back of the room. She wasn't going to give him another chance to be a Gloomy Gus.

"Hi, Diana!" Carolyn called.

"Hi!" she called back, smiling at the child.

Diana was surprised when David kissed Carolyn's cheek, turned her in the direction of the clothing closet, and walked towards her. Her heart raced, but she kept her expression bland. "Good morning, Mr. Jordan."

"Ah...morning." He ran a hand through his hair and shifted his weight from one foot to the other and stared at her. She stared back. "Is there something I can do for you, Mr. Jordan?"

"Ah...no... well actually...yeah. No." He shook his head.

Which was it? "Having a bad day?" she asked.

He sighed. "I just wanted to thank you for spending the day with Carolyn on Saturday. It meant a lot to her."

So she'd spent the day with Carolyn, but not him? She flashed him a meaningless smile. "I enjoyed spending the day with Carolyn. Too bad you couldn't have joined us, Mr. Jordan."

He shifted his gaze to a spot just to the left of her face. "That came out all wrong."

"I doubt it."

"Ah...so...I'd better get going to work."

She nodded. "Goodbye."

"So I'll see you around."

"Where?"

His brought his gaze back to hers. "Here."

"Ah huh. Well," she flashed him another meaningless smile. "Y'all have a nice day. You hear?"

He nodded and walked away.

Way to go, Diana. Real smooth.

"Diana? What did my daddy want just now?"

She turned to smile at Carolyn. "He just said thank you for Saturday." She studied Carolyn's face. "Sweetie? What's wrong? You look sad."

"I can't tell you," she sighed and walked away.

Diana stared after her, hard pressed not to follow her. She reminded herself that Carolyn was but one of many under her care. It wasn't fair to the other children to concentrate so much of her attention on Carolyn.

Diana kept herself busy through the week by throwing her energies into her work. One of the five full-time daycare workers was out sick, so there was a lot to keep her occupied. She spent Monday and Tuesday night visiting the sick and elderly from their church. Wednesday night, she went to choir practice.

By Thursday, it was clear that David wasn't going to call her, much less ask her out. He'd never implied that he had any interest in her. She had no reason to hope for anything from him. Still, she had, and it took a long time to get to sleep that night.

Diana spent valuable time on Friday morning agonizing over what to wear to the picnic. Should she wear her usual coveralls or the new pale pink, midi-length, two-piece dress she'd bought a week earlier? "What do you think, Becki?"

"You look great in pink. Wear it and let him see what he's missing," she said as she and Diana shared an early morning cup of tea before opening the daycare.

Diana had allowed her desire to get to know David, coupled with Becki's encouragement, to get out of hand. She was now firmly in control again. "I told you he wasn't interested."

"That was before you spent the day with him and Carolyn."

"Well, I saw him Monday morning, and nothing had changed. He's so not interested that he implied I'd only spent the day with Carolyn. That's fine. He's not exactly the life of the party. I'm wearing the coveralls," she said.

"But Di, you need to let him see you at your best."

"As far as he's concerned, I don't have a best." She shrugged. "And I'm okay with that."

"You're giving up too easily, Di," Becki objected. "There could be lots of reasons he hasn't called you."

She nodded. "Yeah. The main one being his lack of interest in me." She pushed her cup aside and stood up. "I've made up my mind, Becki. Time spent trying to attract him is wasted time. I should have known that the moment I saw he was still wearing his wedding ring." She glanced at the kitchen clock. "It's time we got downstairs."

"Okay. Okay. You're not going to change. Then I will."

With her hand on the kitchen door, Diana looked over her shoulder at Becki. As usual, she was wearing a chic, washable silk warm-up suit that did wonders for her tall, shapely figure. "What?"

"I'll change too. Give me a pair of coveralls."

She was touched. "Oh, Becki, you don't have to do that."

Becki shrugged. "That's what friends are for. Huh?"

"Oh, Becki! You're great!"

"Yeah," Becki said grinning. "Tell me about it."

"But you are not changing into coveralls."

Chapter Five

"Daddy! Daddy! You came!"

Diana heard Carolyn's scream of pleasure and looked up from the grill where she turned hot dogs. David Jordan walked across the lawn.

Immediately she regretted her refusal to wear something pretty enough to draw his gaze toward her and keep it there. Why hadn't she worn the pink dress?

Becki walked over to her. "I don't think you should give up so easily," Becki whispered in her ear. "Look at him. Even dressed casually, he's gorgeous."

She pulled her gaze away from David to look at Becki. She had to take several deep breaths before she could speak in a normal voice. "He's not interested in me, but there's nothing stopping you from taking a run at him."

Becki took a step backwards, as if Diana had attempted to slap her. "What?! What do you take me for? Do you really think I'd make a play for him knowing how you feel about him?"

"How I...I...don't feel any particular way about him. If you're interested in him, go for it," she said lightly, while part of her died inside at the thought of the beautiful, svelte Becki going after him.

"Oh, Di! You don't have to pretend with me or fear that I will do anything to attract him. I won't. You know I won't."

Before she could respond, out of the corner of her eye, she saw Carolyn practically dragging her father in their direction.

"Oh, no!" She thrust the fork she held at Becki. "Here. I...I have to go inside to get the mustard."

Becki glanced over her shoulder at one of the picnic tables they'd set up on the front lawn. "The mustard's on the table."

"It won't be enough," she said a little wildly and started toward the house. She was not in the mood to face David Jordan.

"Diana! Diana! Where are you going?"

She made it to the side door before Carolyn's voice reached her. A quick glance over her shoulder revealed that Carolyn had let go of her father's hand and was running after her.

She raised her eyes and found David watching her. He was dressed in a pair of dark casual slacks and an open-necked white shirt. Men didn't come any more attractive than him. Or any more unavailable.

Carolyn tugged on her hand.

She looked down into the child's troubled face. It was an effort to smile. "I'm just going to get some mus...something from inside."

"But my daddy's here, Diana."

"Yes, I know." She squeezed Carolyn's hand. "Why don't you go back and keep your daddy company? Make sure he feels welcome."

"Are you going to come speak to him?"

"Of course I will. Maybe not right away, but..."

"Why not? Don't you like him?"

"Yes, I do," she admitted. "I do like your father." That was her problem. No matter how hard she tried not to, she liked him all too well. "But honey, I don't think he likes me."

"Yes he does!" Carolyn said fiercely. "He just doesn't know it yet."

"But you do?"

She nodded eagerly. "Yeah. He's my daddy. I've known him all my life."

Diana laughed. "Do you think he'll mind if you come inside and help me?"

Carolyn glanced over her shoulder. "Diana and I will be right back to make you feel welcome, Daddy!" she bellowed.

Diana laughed again, and they went inside, hand in hand.

David frowned as he watched Carolyn go inside with Diana. Carolyn liked the woman far too much for his peace of mind. He wished Carolyn wasn't so attached to her, but there didn't seem to be much he could do to change that.

He sighed. Of course he understood Carolyn's attachment to her, since he himself found it difficult to stop thinking about her. He kept recalling the comforting sound of her voice and laughter. Worse, he kept seeing the warmth and promise in her eyes when she looked at him. More, he felt it reaching out to surround him with a sense of belonging that he hadn't felt since that awful day of Harriet's accident.

"Hello, Carolyn's father."

He looked up to see a tall, slender, attractive woman coming toward him across the grass. She was smiling, and her hand was extended. She was wearing a pair of white coveralls similar to the ones Diana wore.

"Ms. Howard." He nodded politely.

"Diana and I are so glad you could come, Mr. Jordan. Carolyn's been looking forward to having you here today. She's a very sweet, well-mannered child. You must be very proud of her." She glanced around the yard. "Where is she?"

"She's inside with Di—Ms. Stuart."

"That figures. It's nearly impossible to keep her away from Diana." She smiled and sank down on the grass beside him. "They bonded from day one. But I guess you already know that. I understand you've finally met Diana."

He nodded. "Yes, I have."

"Then you know why Carolyn's so crazy about her."

Great. Another matchmaker. "Excuse me?"

"You know Diana's an absolute delight. She's pretty, sweet, even-tempered, and a great cook. She's everything a man could want." She gave him a coy look. "You're a man. What do you think?"

Clearly, she didn't believe in beating around the bush. Had Diana put her friend up to singing her praises? He was aware of a sense of disappointment. Somehow he'd expected more from Diana. Besides, it wasn't necessary.

"Have I embarrassed you, Mr. Jordan?"

"No," he said slowly. "And call me David."

"Sure thing, David, and I'm Becki." She smiled at him. "I suppose you know that Diana isn't married or seeing anyone special."

"So I understand," he said in a cool voice he hoped would deter her from any more personal remarks.

"But I wouldn't count on things staying that way," she went on. "You see how it is with her. Someone is bound to snatch her up before long. If I were you, I wouldn't wait —"

"I think you've made your point, Ms. Howard."

"Oh, good." She grinned at him. "I was beginning to run out of things to say. So can I interest you in a hot dog?"

He nodded. Becki Gordon's nonstop chatter was enough to give a man a royal headache. "Why not?"

She smiled. "Then follow me."

They rose and moved over to the grill. They topped hot dogs with relish and mustard and then sat on the grass under the shade of a tree. "So tell me, David, what do you do for a living?"

"I'm fortunate enough to have two jobs I enjoy. I'm a CPA. During tax season, I do taxes on the side. The rest of the year, I'm a construction foremen."

"And you're a widower."

He nodded, swallowed hard and looked briefly away. "Yes."

"That must be very hard on both you and Carolyn. I can tell by the way she clings to Diana that she really misses her mom."

He bit into his hot dog. He chewed in silence for several moments before swallowing and turning to look at her through narrowed eyes. "Of course she misses her mother. We both do."

"And it's none of my business?" She didn't wait for him to respond before she went on. "I know that. And I'm not trying to be nosy, I'm—"

"No? Perhaps it's just seems that way to me."

She laughed. "You're right. I shouldn't poke my nose where it doesn't belong. I just thought you should know that...well, Diana is a lovely person. The best part is she's very available. But with everything she has to offer, she won't be for long. I wouldn't leave it too long, if I were you. But I've already told you that."

"Yes," he agreed shortly. "You've already made that point."

"Oh, well." She shrugged. "You know what they say about repetition being the mother of retention."

The woman was impossible. "I'll keep that in mind," he said wearily.

"Daddy!"

He was relieved to see Carolyn and Diana emerge from the house. Carolyn ran over to them. Her gaze went from him to Becki and back to him. "What are you doing, Daddy?"

"Eating a hot dog."

"No. What are you doing with Becki?" Carolyn demanded.

He stared at Carolyn in surprise.

"He's not doing anything, Carolyn," Becki said, springing to her feet. "We were actually talking about what a nice person Diana is."

A smile replaced Carolyn's frown. "Oh. That's all right, then."

Becki ruffled her hair. "Yes, it is. I'm outta here."

Finally, David thought thankfully.

Carolyn tugged on his free hand in hers.

He looked at her.

"Daddy, aren't you going to come say hello to Diana?"

Diana stood laughing with two other parents on the other side of the lawn. His eagerness to speak to her surprised him. "Sure, sweetie." He finished his hot dog and got to his feet.

Carolyn smiled up at him. "She'll be glad to see you, Daddy. She likes you and she thinks you're handsome."

"Yeah?"

"Yeah."

He smiled down at her. "Let's go say hello to your Diana."

She slipped her hands in his. "She could be your Diana, if you wanted her to, Daddy."

He squeezed her hand gently. "Let's not go there again."

She tugged at his hand. "Oh, all right. Come on, Daddy."

"Okay, sweetie," he said, trying to ignore the butterflies in his stomach. "Lead the way."   Diana turned before they reached her. For a moment he thought he saw a look of delight in her eyes as her gaze met his. It was gone so fast that he wasn't sure it had ever really been there.

"Hi Mrs. Smith and Mrs. Rhodes," Carolyn said to the two women with Diana.

David smiled at the two women. "Hi. I'm David Jordan."

Carolyn barely waited for the women's response before turning her attention to Diana. "I've bought my Daddy to say hello to you, Diana."

"I'll bet you're as eager to talk to Diana as Carolyn is to have you talk to her," Mrs. Rhodes said, smiling at him. She slipped her arm through Mrs. Smith. "Let's go see what our darlings are up to."

"Here's my Daddy, Diana," Carolyn said again.

He looked down at Diana. "How are you?"

She smiled without meeting his gaze. "Fine. You?"

"Okay."

Now that he was close to her, he was aware of a feeling of excitement. He liked being with her as much as Carolyn did.

"It means a lot to Carolyn to have you here today." She motioned toward the table. "Please help yourself to anything you like. Enjoy now."

He watched her walk away, suppressing the desire to follow. He'd actually taken several steps after her when he realized what he was doing and stopped.

"Daddy? Why are you stopping? Aren't you going to go after her?"

He sighed. "No."

"Daddy? You didn't like Becki more than Diana. Did you?"

He took Carolyn's hand in his and led her to the tree where he'd been sitting with Becki Howard. "Ms. Howard seems very nice, but I'm not interested in her."

"Oh, good," she said and threw her arms around his neck.

I was afraid you'd like her better than Diana."

He hugged her. "Well, I don't."

"Good." She sat next to him. "Want to share a hot dog, Daddy?"

"Yes, sweetie."

They finished the hot dog together and shared an orange soda. He kept expecting Diana to come back over to talk to them. Not only did she keep her distance, but he couldn't see that she even looked in his direction again. It wasn't until he and Carolyn were ready to leave at four o'clock that she came to say goodbye.

"Are you mad at Daddy and me, Diana?" Carolyn demanded.

The question seemed to surprise her. "Oh, honey, no! Of course not."

"Then why didn't you spend any time with us? We waited and waited, but you didn't come to sit with us. Why?"

David found himself almost holding his breath, waiting for her response.

She shrugged in an offhand manner that he found annoying. "You and I spend a lot of time together. I thought you and your daddy would want to be alone," she said lightly. She smiled at Carolyn. "Have a great weekend, honey. See you Monday."

"Okay. You too."

"Thanks, honey." Her smile vanished as she nodded in his general direction. "Thanks for coming. Bye!" She walked away without waiting for his reply.

He stared after her. What had happened to the warm, funny woman with whom he and Carolyn had spent a delightful afternoon at the park?

"I don't think she likes you anymore, Daddy."

David tore his gaze away from Diana's retreating figure to look down at Carolyn. "I'm sorry. What did you say, sweetie?"

"Diana. Aren't you listening, Daddy? She says she does, but she acts like she doesn't like you anymore."

He shrugged, trying to project a nonchalance he didn't feel. He scooped Carolyn up in his arms and hugged her. "Never mind. As long as you like me, that's all that matters." Even as he spoke, he knew he wasn't being honest. He did care whether or not Diana Stuart liked or disliked him. He needed to decide if he were prepared to do anything about it.

Chapter Six

"You want to talk about it?"

Diana tied the last plastic trash bag securely, carried it to the side of the house, and tossed it into the dumpster. She glanced around the front yard. No more balloons or party favors were scattered on the lawn. Everything was just as it had been that morning before the picnic.

"We need to talk, Diana."

She turned to face Becki, who stood at the open side door with her hands on her hips. Even in those baggy coveralls, Becki looked chic and attractive. Of course, David had noticed her. She couldn't blame him. Or Becki, who'd done her best to look as unattractive as possible.

"Diana!"

"No need to shout, Becki," she said lightly, giving the lawn one final glance. "I heard you, but what's to talk about?"

Becki turned and followed Diana as she squeezed past her on her way inside. "Nothing, but I get the feeling you think there is."

Diana closed and locked the front door of the center before turning to face Becki again. "Look, I was the one who told you to go after him. I'm not going to complain now that you have." She bit her lip. "I hope you two will ... well, you know."

Becki shook her head. "No, I don't know! You're carrying on as if I'd gone behind your back and got a date with him."

"It wasn't behind my back." She pushed herself away from the door. "Now, what about a cup of tea before you go?" She started for the back of the house where a locked staircase lead up to the apartments above the daycare. She half hoped Becki would refuse. No such luck. She heard Becki behind her on the stairs.

Inside her apartment, she put on the tea kettle. She could feel Becki's eyes burning into her back. "I wasn't trying to steal him from you, Diana."

She turned to face Becki. "He isn't mine to steal."

"Diana! Will you shut up long enough to listen to me? I'm not interested in him, and he's not interested in me. We talked about you."

Diana pressed her hands against her hot cheeks. "I'm sorry, Becki. It's just that the two of you looked so perfect."

"Granted, your David is attractive. However, I happen to be seeing someone already, thank you very much. But even if I weren't, I would never go after him when I know how you feel."

"You're seeing someone?" The kettle began boiling. Diana set two cups on the table and carried the kettle to the table.

Becki had already slipped the tea bags into the cups. Diana poured water over them and resumed her seat. "Who? Details, Becki. Give me details."

Becki grinned at her. "I met him at the supermarket two months ago."

"Two whole months? Why haven't I heard about him?"

Becki added sugar to her cup. "Our relationship is so new. I didn't want to...well, you know. I wanted to really get settled with him before I talked about him."

Diana took an appreciative sip from her cup. "Tell me more. What's his name?"

"Paul Hamilton Mitchell."

"And what does Paul Hamilton Mitchell do for a living?"

"He's a buyer for a department store. He's never been married and he's a great guy." Becki's eyes sparkled. "I really like him, Di." She shrugged. "The only downer is that he's sort of religious."

Diana's smile vanished. She put down her cup. "How is his being religious a downer?"

"Oh, don't look at me like that. I just meant he'll soon be expecting me to go to church with him."

"And that would be a bad thing because...?"

"I didn't say it was bad," Becki denied. "I'm just not ready to go all devout. When you do, there are so many things you can't do."

"When you are devout, you won't want to do those things," Diana corrected. "There's a difference." She propped her elbows on the table. "You didn't tell me what he said about me? David Jordan, I mean."

Becki looked disappointed. "Nothing really. He didn't have time. First I had to work my way up to telling him what a great catch you were. When I had, Carolyn came charging over demanding to know what he was doing with me. That child is absolutely crazy about you."

"The feeling is mutual, but David Jordan's not interested in me."

"Oh, I wouldn't be too sure about that. He spent most of the day watching you."

"So he likes to watch me. So what? So far it's gotten me absolutely nowhere fast with him."

"Things can and do change."

"Maybe so, but who says I want them to?" She picked up her cup and sipped her tea. "We have absolutely nothing in common."

"Come on, Di. You don't mean that."

She nodded. "I do."

"Having second thoughts because he's white?"

"No. I'm having second thoughts about wasting my time daydreaming about a man who's not interested in me. Life's too short and to full for that."

"And his being white?"

"Has nothing to do with anything."

"Do you think it's an issue for him?"

Diana shook her head. "No, I don't."

Diana lay on a chaise lounge with her eyes closed, enjoying the warm starlit night on the small balcony outside her living room. Earlier, she had prayed for the strength to forget David Jordan. Now, she just wanted to work in harmony with her prayers by not thinking about him. Just at the moment, it wasn't working.

She jumped when the phone shattered the calmness of the night. She sat up, reaching for the handset, which lay at the end of the lounge. "Hello," she said.

"Hello, Diana. This is Gloria Jordan."

"Mrs. Jordan?" Why would Carolyn's grandmother be calling her at nine o'clock on a Friday night? "What can I do for you?"

"I know it's rather late for a social call."

She released a deep breath she hadn't realized she was holding. "A social call?"

"Yes, dear. I won't keep you long. I just wanted to tell you how being at the center with you has really helped Carolyn. She's no longer withdrawn and sad."

"That's very kind of you to say, Mrs. Jordan, but—"

"I'm not being kind. And dear, please call me Gloria."

"Oh. Well, thank you, Gloria, but I'm not the only one Carolyn interacts with at the daycare. Becki Howard is—"

"Yes, yes, dear. I know Ms. Howard is a dear, but you're the one who's been so instrumental in helping Carolyn. And I'm so grateful. I'd like to do something to show my appreciation."

"That's very kind, but not necessary. Anything I may have done for her, I've enjoyed doing."

"Oh, how sweet, but it would mean a lot to me if you'd let me do something for you. Why don't you come to dinner sometime? As you know, I'm a widow and I live alone. I'm sometimes lonely. Won't you extend some of the kindness you've shown Carolyn to me?"

There was no way she wanted to spend another day in David Jordan's company. "That's sounds very nice," she began. "but—"

"How about Sunday at three?" Gloria interrupted.

Diana blinked. "Sunday. This Sunday?"

"I thought the two of us could have a nice dinner and talk a little."

Just the two of them? She relaxed. "I'll be in church until early afternoon. I'll be free around four, but my car is in the shop so I'll have to get a ride there and back."

"Four is just fine, dear. If you can manage to find a ride here, I'll drive you home."

"Okay. Can I bring anything? A meat? A vegetable dish?"

"Just yourself, dear. I plan to spoil you a little."

She smiled, touched. "I'll come prepared to be spoiled."

"Oh, dear, did you have to wear jeans?"

David stared at his mother in surprise as he closed her kitchen door behind him and Carolyn. "That's an unusual greeting, Mom." He bent to kiss her cheek. He straightened and inhaled deeply. "Something smells finger-licking good."

"I've a baked chicken and a ham in the oven, dear," she answered, staring at him through narrowed eyes. "Oh, dear, I really think you have a bad case of five o'clock shadow. I wished you'd shaved before you came."

"I never shave on Sundays and I always wear jeans."

She nodded, looking unhappy. "I'd forgotten, otherwise I'd have reminded you to shave when I called."

"Why? It's not as if we have company." He paused, looking around the kitchen. The big, mahogany table where the three of them usually ate Sunday dinner wasn't set. "Do you want me and Carolyn to lay the table?"

"The table in the dining room is already laid," she said as she checked her pots on the stove. "And actually, dear, we do have company."

He opened his mouth to ask who, but suddenly he knew who her guest was. He turned to look at his mother. "Mom! You didn't."

She met his gaze. "Didn't what?"

"Didn't what?" Carolyn repeated. "What didn't Granny do?"

"Nothing, dear."

"She knows," David said coolly.

His mother smiled sweetly at him. "Why don't you go into the living room and say hello to our guest? I'll keep Carolyn here to help me."

"And what if I'm not in the mood to do that, Mom?"

"I didn't raise you to be rude. You'll go say hello," she said confidently.

He bit back the response trembling on his lips as he turned on his heel. There was nothing to stop him from collecting Carolyn and leaving. Nothing, that is, except his desire to see Diana Stuart again.

As he had known, she was in the living room. She wore a pretty, soft pink dress with a full skirt that swirled around her calves as she swayed in time to the classical music filling the air. The heels she wore highlighted her legs, which were very nice.

Her eyes were closed so she wasn't aware of him. He stood in the doorway, unable to look away from her. Her movements were as graceful and sweeping as a dancer's. His gaze shifted to her hands. He imagined them caressing his cheeks as she leaned in to touch her mouth to his.

She opened her eyes suddenly, saw him, gasped, and came to an abrupt stop. "Mr. Jordan! I ... I didn't hear you. How ... how long have you been standing there?"

He found her breathless voice rather attractive. How would it sound whispering something soft and sweet to him?

"Only for a few moments."

"Why didn't you say something?"

"I didn't want to startle you." Noting how lovely she looked, he suddenly wished he had shaved and worn a pair of dress pants.

"And yet you did."

"Sorry." He strolled into the room. "My mother sent me to entertain you while she and Carolyn finish dinner."

"Oh."

"Can I get you anything?"

She shook her head. "Ah, no. I had some of your mother's excellent lemonade ten minutes ago."

For a moment, they stood in silence, staring at each other.

"I didn't expect to see you here. I understood from your mother that it would be just the two of us for dinner."

"And I thought it would be just Mom, Carolyn and me."

She looked dismayed. "Oh. Then you wouldn't have come if you known I'd be here."

He shook his head. "I didn't say that."

"You didn't need to. I know how you feel." She glanced over her shoulder toward the kitchen. "I wish your mother had told me you'd be here." She sounded and looked irritated.

"I get the feeling you wouldn't have come if you'd known Carolyn and I would be here."

Her response was quick and ego deflating. "You're right. I wouldn't have come."

He frowned. "Why not?"

She stared at him, her dark eyes narrowed. "I think you know the answer to that question."

"No, I don't."

"I'm sure you can figure it out with a little effort. In the meantime, I'm going home."

"No!" The word was forced out of his mouth before he could stop it.

She stared at him. "What?"

"You're here now, and Mom is sure to have cooked enough food for at least ten people."

"Maybe so, but this isn't what I expected when I agreed to come to dinner." She scooped her handbag up from the sofa. "Would you explain to your mother that I had to go?"

"No, I won't."

She shrugged. "Fine. I'll explain myself the next time I see her." She left the living room.

He could hear her heels clinking on the tiles in the hallway. Moments later, he heard her struggling to open the deadbolt lock on the front door.

He left the living room and rushed down the hall to the front door.

She turned to face him. "Would you help me with the door? I can't seem to figure out how to unlock it."

"I think you've misunderstood. I—"

"Are you going to unlock the door for me?"

He shook his head. "Not until you hear me out."

She turned back to the door, stared at both locks in silence for several moments, and finally managed to get the door open. She quickly went through, closing it behind herself.

He pulled the door open.

In her haste to get away from him, she was practically running down the sidewalk.

"Diana! Wait!" He followed her out of the house. Uncaring of the neighbors sitting on front porches watching, he reached out, caught her hand in his, and bought her to a reluctant stop. He turned her to face him. The sight of tears in her eyes stunned him. "Hey! Don't cry."

She tugged at her hand. "Let go."

He softened his voice. "I will. I just want you to understand."

"There's nothing to understand, Mr. Jordan." Her voice shook, but she stared defiantly up at him.

"I think there is. You seem to think that I don't like you," he began slowly, nonplused by her tears. Why couldn't women play fair? Why did they always have to resort to tears?

She tugged at her hand again. Instead of releasing it, he cradled it in his, rubbing the ball of his thumb across the back of her hand. "I wish you'd let me explain."

"There's nothing to explain. I knew the moment we met that I wasn't the type of woman you'd be attracted to. And I am painfully aware that a lot of men don't like women my size. You're obviously one of them."

"You don't know enough about me to say that!" he said, stung by her less than flattering assessment of his character. She made him sound like an immature boy who didn't know that beauty was only skin deep.

"I know enough to know that I don't want to know anymore," she said in a biting voice.

He dropped her hand. "I'm sorry to hear that, because I've known for some time now that I don't know nearly as much about you as I'd like to," he was stunned to hear himself admit.

She stared up at him. "I...what?"

"And it might interest you to know that I find you very attractive. Even when you're wearing those ridiculous coveralls." He allowed his gaze to flick briefly over her. "And especially when you're wearing pink."

Chapter Seven

Diana didn't believe him. She didn't want to. She was past caring what he thought of her. She'd made her peace. So why was her heart beating so furiously? And why was she eagerly awaiting his next words?

"Look, Diana, I know I've been sort of a ... a ..."

"Jerk would be an appropriate word with which to fill in the blank," she said helpfully.

His eyes narrowed slightly and his lips tightened, but he nodded. "Okay. I've been a jerk. Satisfied? Now come back inside."

Now that was definitely not a good idea. That way laid almost certain heartbreak. There was only one acceptable answer. So why didn't she give it?

It wasn't like her to be so indecisive. Even when he reached out to take her hand in his again, she didn't resist. Instead, her breath caught in her throat. "That's not a good idea," she finally muttered.

"How do you know unless you try it?" He squeezed her hand gently.

She swallowed hard.

"Look, Mom will have told Carolyn you're here. She will be very disappointed if you leave. Worse, she'll blame me."

That's what this was all about! "I see. You want me to come back for Carolyn's sake?" She jerked at her hand.

His grip on her hand tightened. "No! I put that badly. Let me make myself clear. I want you to come back because I want you to come back."

She longed to believe him. Still, wouldn't going back be working out of harmony with her prayer to forget him? She hesitated, biting her lip. Her head urged her to say no and leave. Her heart, with its own ideas, won. "Okay."

He released her hand.

They returned to the house in silence. She was very conscious of him and his subtle cologne. She liked the rugged look of his unshaven face. Back inside the living room, she sat on the sofa. A warm feeling spread through her as he sat beside her, half facing her.

She waited for him to say something. Anything. He didn't oblige. He just sat there staring at her.

"So, Mr. Jor—"

"David."

"David," she repeated, nodding slowly, regaining her confidence. "Nice name. Nice man." *Oh, no, Diana!* she wailed inwardly. *You're flirting with him again!* She almost felt him stiffen beside her. She waited for the withdrawal. Maybe a cutting remark. She turned to face him. "Look, I don't usually go around flirting with men I don't know."

That hadn't come out right. Now he'd think she did flirt with men she did know.

"So you're making an exception in my case?" And when she reluctantly nodded, he smiled. "Good."

Her heart began to pound, and her stomach twisted into knots. Sitting next to him was going to her head. She got to her feet and moved to a single chair. "This is better. Now we can talk. If you want."

"I want," he said softly. He glanced over his shoulder, toward the door which lead toward the back of the house. She vaguely heard Carolyn's laughter, presumably coming from the kitchen. "But not here. Not now."

Was he having second thoughts already? "Then where? When?"

He hesitated. She saw the indecision in his eyes. She waited. He was facing one of the roadblocks he'd put up between them. Was he ready to go around it to meet her halfway?

"I thought maybe we could have dinner."

"When?" She was doing it again. Acting too eager. Not leaving him guessing like her cousin Hank always said a woman should.

"When?"

"Yes. When David?"

"Ah... tomorrow night around seven? What kind of food do you like?"

"You see, David, the trouble is, I like most foods." She surprised herself by laughing. After a moment of silence, he joined in.

"So it's a date then?"

She nodded. "Yes."

"Have you ever been to the Moshulu down at Penn's Landing?" he asked of an old sailing boat that had been turned into a restaurant. "I thought we could have dinner there. Then maybe walk along the pier later, if it's not too cool. Okay?"

She would gladly walk along the pier with him in the midst of a gale force wind if he asked her. However, she thought it best to keep that knowledge to herself. "It sounds great."

"Good." He patted the sofa next to him. "Come sit beside me. I don't bite, you know."

"No? Well, I can't promise I won't bite you." She groaned and closed her eyes briefly. She was hopeless; determined to run him away with overly aggressive behavior.

"I'll take my chances," he said, patting the sofa cushion again.

She resumed her seat next to him. She tingled when he took her hand in his, linking his lean fingers with hers. *Oh, Lord,* she prayed silently. *Show me the way.*

David looked down at their entwined hands. In contrast to his work-roughened, pale fingers, hers was soft, brown, and warm. And yet their linked fingers looked right together. He was surprised at the affect she was having on him. Why should he be so aware of a woman so physically different from the type he preferred?

"Daddy!"

She gently pulled at her hand and he released it and stood up just as Carolyn ran into the room. Carolyn's eyes danced with delight when she saw Diana. "Diana! Why didn't you tell me you were here?"

"It was a surprise," Diana said in her normal, sweet voice.

"I like surprises." Carolyn turned to look at him. "Granny says it's time for dinner."

He turned to look at her. She smiled at him and he smiled back. Still, the look in her eyes gave him an uneasy feeling. Had he been too hasty? He'd meant everything he'd said to get her back inside the house. But just maybe he wasn't ready to jump feet first into a relationship with her. All his instincts told him she wasn't the kind of woman to accept or settle for anything less than a total commitment.

He now had to admit he wanted to get to know her. Nevertheless, he wasn't ready for what she seemed to want. But then he didn't really know what she wanted. He was only making assumptions. "Daddy!"

"What?" he asked, distractedly.

"You're not listening again!" Carolyn complained.

"I'm sorry, sweetie. What did you say?"

Carolyn grinned up at him. "I asked what you were doing in here all alone with Diana."

"Talking."

Carolyn looked disappointed. "Just talking? You weren't kissing or hugging her a little? She's really nice to hug, Daddy. I'll bet she's nice to kiss too. Just like you are."

Aware of Diana watching with an unabashed smile on her face, he felt the back of his neck burning. Just two weeks ago, he would have held her lack of embarrassment against her. Definitely not now.

He scowled down at Carolyn. "That's a very personal question, young lady."

"Well, I'm your very personal daughter, Daddy."

"So you are, but it's none of your business."

"But Daddy, your business is my business," Carolyn insisted.

He laughed, brushing the back of his fingers across her cheek. "Nice try, Sweetcakes."

"Well, let's go eat then." She slipped a hand into his before turning to extend her free one to Diana, who accepted it with a warm smile.

Daddy was doing it again. Staring at Diana. He wasn't talking and he wasn't eating much. And Daddy loved Granny's cooking. Carolyn stifled a happy giggle. Daddy was sitting at the head of the table with Diana on his right, Granny on his left, and her next to Granny. Daddy was going to get a stiff neck if he didn't look at something besides Diana soon.

But she was happy. She'd been praying hard that Daddy would change his mind about Diana. And it had worked! She'd have to be very good and say an extra special prayer to thank the Lord for opening Daddy's eyes.

"So, honey, what would you like to do this Saturday?"

Carolyn sighed happily and turned to look at Granny as she spoke to her. "I don't know." She looked at Daddy. "What are we doing Saturday, Daddy?"

"No. I meant you and me, honey," Granny said. "I haven't had you to myself for a whole day for over a month. I was hoping we could do something together. Just the two of us."

Carolyn giggled. Granny liked to spend what she called "quality time" with her. She liked it too. "What kind of stuff, Granny?"

"Female stuff," Granny said, winking at her. "Can do, honey?"

"Can do, Granny!"

"Good." Granny smiled at Daddy. "What about you, dear? Do you have any plans for Saturday?"

She giggled when Daddy looked at Diana before shrugging. "Nothing at the moment."

"You and Daddy can do something together, Diana!" Carolyn said. "Won't that be fun?"

"Sounds like it," Diana agreed, her gaze on Daddy's face.

Now was Daddy's chance to ask Diana out. She leaned forward in her seat, not wanting to miss a word. But Daddy remained silent. And now, he wasn't even looking at Diana. She slumped back against her seat. What was wrong with Daddy, anyway?

Diana folded her napkin and laid it on the table next to her plate. "That was a lovely meal. Thank you for inviting me."

"Thank you for coming." Granny smiled. "I'm delighted you could join us. I'm sure David and Carolyn feel the same way."

She sat up in her seat, grinning. "We sure do! Don't we, Daddy?"

"It was ... a pleasant surprise," Daddy finally said.

"Well, I'd better be on my way," Diana said.

Without making a date with Daddy! She panicked. She didn't know what to do. She turned to look at Granny.

She felt better when Granny smiled at her before looking at Daddy. "David, dear, I was thinking. Why don't you let Carolyn spend the night here? That way, we can get a head start on that quality time."

"Okay. Thanks, Mom."

Carolyn was surprised and a little hurt at how quickly Daddy agreed. She and Daddy had never spent a night apart since Mommy went to live with the Lord.

"Good. Then you can take Diana home. She lives above the daycare. It's right on your way, dear."

"I can walk with no problem," Diana said quickly. "I don't want to be a bother."

Carolyn frowned. Diana didn't sound as if she wanted to be with Daddy.

"It's no bother," Daddy said, just as quickly.

"Good. Then it's all settled," Granny said.

Daddy looked at her. "Is that all right with you, sweetie?"

It wasn't, but Diana was never going to be her new mommy if she and Daddy didn't spend time alone. She smiled at him. "Yes, Daddy."

Diana's perfume filled the cab of the SUV as David drove her home. For the first time in years, he found himself wishing that he was driving a car instead of a sports utility vehicle.

Harriet had always insisted she didn't mind not having a car. He wondered if Diana minded. But there was an upside to taking her home in his SUV. He got to hold her hand as he helped her out.

He kept her hand in his as he walked her up the driveway.

At the door, she smiled up at him. "Would you like to come in for a cup of coffee?"

"Yes," he said and eagerly followed her up the two flights of stairs to her apartment.

Her apartment was a combination of white walls, deep blue woodwork, long blue and white curtains, and dark blue carpeting. It suited her. "Would you like to hear some music?" She walked over to the stereo in the corner of the big living room. "Do you like jazz?"

He nodded, smiling. He and Harriet had shared most interests, except a taste in music. She'd only tolerated jazz when he was around, and he did the same for easy listening when she was around. "I love it."

"There! You see," she said as if she had finally proven a much disputed point after a protracted argument. "We already have something in common."

He stared at her. When she smiled like that, she was all dark warmth and beauty. "You mean in addition to a mutual physical attraction?"

Her smile vanished.

He raked a hand through his hair. Had his careless remark made her think he was one of those blockheads who turned every outing into a wrestling match? "I didn't mean that the way it must have sounded," he said quickly. "I'll never overstep any bounds you set."

The tension left her shoulders and she smiled again. "Oh, David. I didn't think that."

"You didn't? Good. I wouldn't want you to think you couldn't trust me."

"Of course, I trust you, David. Now that that's settled, here's a really big question."

"Okay," he said cautiously. "Shoot. I can handle it."

"Okay. Here goes. I know some men really hate this, but I'm going to ask it anyway."

"All right," he said wearily, certain her question was going to put him on the spot.

"Okay. You don't mind instant coffee? Do you?"

He stared at her in surprise, then laughed. "No." He was beginning to think he wouldn't mind much of anything about Diana Stuart.

"Good."

They exchanged warm smiles.

"Put on any of the CD's there, have a seat, and I'll be right back," she told him.

Ten minutes later they were sitting on the big, blue sofa along one wall, drinking coffee and listening to Miles Davis. He felt relaxed, content to just sit next to her.

"Carolyn's a beautiful little girl," she said suddenly. "Does she... take after her mother?"

The question snapped David out of his reverie. He didn't want to talk about Harriet with Diana. He nodded, glanced at his watch, and rose. "It's getting late. I should be going."

She blinked up at him. "Did I say something I shouldn't have?"

"No. Of course not. I just thought since Carolyn's staying with Mom, I'd go home and..." And what? Think about Diana? Feel guilty for wanting to be with her?

When he didn't respond, she rose.

He stepped back.

"Are you...I know it hasn't been long since your wife died—"

"She didn't die," he said sharply. "She was killed. There's a difference."

"I know. I'm sorry, David."

She reached out a hand to touch his arm, but he shook his head and turned away. "I have to go."

"David! Wait a minute. Please."

He turned back to face her. The distress on her face was clear. He was an idiot. "Look, I'm sorry," he said, wanting to make things right with her. "If you could just bear with me for awhile. This is all so new. When I married Harriet, I expected to spend the rest of my life with her. I have to get used to dating all over again."

She inclined her head slightly.

He brushed his fingers against the back of her hand. "I'll see you tomorrow night. That is, if I haven't scared you off."

She flashed him a brief smile. "No such luck."

He stared down into her eyes. Her expression was open and honest. He would always know where he stood with her. "I'm glad to hear that. I'll try not to make it too hard on you."

"I'll hold you to that," she said quietly.

He nodded. "I'm sure you will."

"Y'all know I will."

He probably owed her an explanation, but he wasn't up to it just yet. He sighed. "I...I don't want to scare you off."

She flashed him a brief, reassuring smile. "It'll take more than a little bad temper to scare me off."

"Good. I'll call you." He resisted the urge to lean down to kiss her mouth, squeezed her hand gently, and let himself out of her apartment.

Chapter Eight

David called his mother as soon as he got home. "Can you keep Carolyn overnight tomorrow?"

"Oh, David! Dear, you're taking her out."

"Yes," he admitted reluctantly, perching on the edge of his recliner. Now she would hit him with a barrage of questions and unwanted suggestions.

"I'd be glad to have Carolyn for another night and when she finds out why you're —"

"I'd just as soon she didn't find out, Mom."

"But why, dear? It would make her very happy."

He sat back in his chair in the darkened living room. "I don't want to get her hopes up. I'm taking Diana out to dinner. It's not as if I'm interested in marrying her."

"David! What are you suggesting? That you're seeing Diana without any intentions of...she's a devout Christian!"

He sighed. "Right now I just know I want to see her, but I have no intentions of hurting her or..."

"Or what? David, she's serious about you. You must know that. It's obvious every time she looks at you. It would be so easy for you to hurt her."

"I'm not going to hurt her, Mom, and I don't want Carolyn to know about our date."

"It's your decision, David, but I think you're making a mistake. About not telling Carolyn and seeing Diana without any serious interest."

He sighed. He knew that frosty tone. "I'd never do anything to compromise her faith. You seem to forget that I'm a Christian, too."

"No, David, you're the one who's been forgetting that lately," she reminded him.

"If I have, I've been given ample reason to!" he said. "I played by the rules! I didn't sleep around. I married the woman I loved! I didn't drink or gamble. We taught Carolyn to know and love God, and where did it get me? I lost the most important person in my life. And for what? What did I do to deserve that? What did she do? We did everything that was required of us. Why did it happen to me? To her? To us? Why not to some...some godless person who never cared about what God required of him? Why is she dead?"

"Oh, David!" Her voice cracked and he knew she was fighting back tears. "You've read the account of Job's suffering and you know that being a Christian is not a guarantee that bad things won't happen to us or to those we love."

"Then maybe there's no point in being one!"

"Oh, David! How can you say such a thing?"

There was no mistaking the sob in her voice this time. "Don't cry, Mom. Please. I'm not saying I don't believe in God anymore. I'm just having a little problem working things out. I need a little more time."

"Then maybe you should wait to take Diana out."

"No. No. Wanting to take her out is one of the few things I'm sure of."

"Come back home, David, and we'll pray together."

While Harriet lay in the hospital in a coma for two weeks, he'd prayed. Incessantly. Fervently. She'd died anyway. "Mom, you pray for me, if it'll make you feel better."

"You're not coming."

"No."

"I know it's late, but I need to talk to you."

Diana knew the moment she heard Gloria Jordan's voice on the phone that something was wrong. She turned off the movie she'd been watching and pushed her recliner into the upright position. "I'm listening."

"David told me he'd asked you out. Before you go, I think there's something you should know about him and Harriet."

"Okay," she said slowly. "I'll ask him."

"He won't want to talk about their relationship."

That much she knew. "Then I probably don't need to know right now. I appreciate your willingness to tell me, but if he doesn't want me to know about them, I'll wait until he does."

"Oh, dear. You are a treasure. I didn't intend to break any of his confidences. I just want to tell you that he's still having a hard time accepting Harriet's death. He won't be too easy to get along with right now, but if you can hang in there for awhile, he's well worth knowing... and loving."

The loving part she already had down. That left the knowing part. "I can be patient, if that's what he needs."

"He needs that and a lot of love. He's really hurting now, and there's nothing I can do to help him except pray for him. I'm hoping you can do more."

After they said their goodnights, Diana got down on her knees and prayed for a long time before she went to bed that night. She lay sleepless for what seemed like hours. Gloria's call had unnerved her in a way she couldn't explain.

What had David said to his mother to trigger that call to her? And what had his mother wanted to tell her? Had she made a mistake by not listening? It was all well and good to be noble, but if David chose not to tell her things she needed to know, where would that leave her? Them? Or any relationship they might hope to have together? If he didn't feel that he could talk to her, would they even have a relationship at all?

She remembered that he'd said they shared not a mutual liking, but a mutual physical attraction. It was much more than that for her. Was she equal to the challenge of making it more for him?

Diana couldn't decide if she should tell Becki about her date with David. In the end, she decided not to. She felt mean, but she didn't feel up to answering all the questions Becki was sure to bombard her with if she knew.

Carolyn was another matter. The moment Gloria and she arrived the next afternoon, she rushed across the room to throw her arms around Diana's legs. "Diana! Hello, Diana!"

"Hiya, sweetie!" She leaned down to give Carolyn a quick squeeze before straightening to face Gloria. Gloria smiled, but Diana saw the worried look in the blue eyes so like David's. "Good morning, dear."

"Good morning, Gloria." She smiled down at Carolyn. "Sweetie, why don't you go take your jacket off and put your lunch box away?"

"Okay." Carolyn unwrapped her arms from Diana and threw herself at Gloria for a hug. "Goodbye, Granny."

"Goodbye, darling. Have a great afternoon."

Gloria turned to smile at her. "I hope you enjoy your evening, dear."

Diana felt the blood rush to her cheeks and hoped that Becki, sitting across the room, couldn't hear over the noise of the children playing. "Thanks."

"Well. I'll see you later, dear." She waved at Carolyn and left.

"Diana, can I ask you something?"

She glanced down to find Carolyn at her side. "Of course."

"Did my daddy kiss you when he took you home last night?"

"No, he didn't."

"Then why didn't you kiss him?"

She suppressed a smile. That would have gone over real well with David. "Because your father wouldn't have liked that."

Carolyn blinked up at her. "Who told you that? Daddy loves to be kissed. Me and Granny kiss him all the time."

Diana kneeled beside Carolyn. "I'm sure you're right, but we really don't know each other well enough for that."

Carolyn frowned. "How long will it take before you know him well enough to kiss him?"

"Carolyn! Come play with me!" A small voice demanded.

Both Carolyn and Diana turned to see Susie Howard sitting on the floor several feet away, playing with a 3-D jigsaw puzzle.

"Go ahead, sweetie," Diana said eagerly.

"Oh. All right," Carolyn said and skipped across the room to join Susie.

She sighed, knowing Carolyn, she knew her reprieve was only momentary. She walked across to the desk, just as the phone rang. She lifted the receiver. "Good afternoon. Happy Time Daycare. Diana Stuart speaking."

"Hi Diana."

Against the backdrop of muted sounds of machinery, she recognized David's deep, warm voice immediately. She sank down onto the chair behind the desk. Her heart was pounding, but she was proud of how steady her voice was. "Oh. David. Hello."

"I called to remind you of our date tonight."

As if she could forget it. "Well, I'm glad you did because I clean forgot all about it," she teased.

"You did?"

He sounded as nervous as she felt. Which served to endear him to her even more while increasing her own comfort level. "No, of course not. I'm only teasing."

"Oh! Well...ah...good! Last night, I was—I'm sorry I wasn't..."

"Last night doesn't matter," she said quietly.

"Okay. So. Then. I'll see you later?"

"Yes."

"Good. I...I'm...looking forward to tonight."

She smiled. "So am I."

"Ah...so...bye."

"Goodbye." She put the phone down and realized that the noise level in the room had greatly decreased. And both Becki and Carolyn were staring at her.

For a moment she wasn't sure why. Granted she had smiled like the proverbial Cheshire cat when David told her he was looking forward to their date, but neither Carolyn nor Becki could have known who she was talking to. Unless... she groaned silently as she recalled herself clearly calling him David.

"That was my daddy!" Carolyn accused, bounding to her feet. "Why didn't you let me talk to him?"

"It was? What's going on here?" Becki demanded, right behind Carolyn.

Diana groaned inwardly and prepared herself for the onslaught of indignant questions.

She waited until they were both standing in front of the desk before she spoke. "He didn't ask to speak to you, Carolyn."

"Then what did he want?"

She opened her mouth, then quickly closed it. David probably wanted to tell Carolyn about their date himself. "We needed to discuss something that had nothing to do with you," she said. Hopefully she didn't sound as guilty as she felt.

Carolyn's eyes narrowed and she stared at Diana with a disbelieving look on her face. "Are you sure?"

"Yes," she said calmly. "I'm sure."

"Well. All right, but you could have let me talk to him. I'm not going to see him until tomorrow night. Granny told me this morning that he had something to do and I'm to spend another night with her. I don't like it when we don't see each other every day."

"I didn't know," she said. "But he was calling from work so he didn't really have much time to talk."

Carolyn shot her an angry look before going back to play with Susie.

Becki parked herself on the side of the desk. "Isn't there something you want to tell me?" she demanded in a hurt voice.

Diana glanced across the room to find Carolyn watching her. This wasn't right. She shouldn't be hiding things and lying by omission to the important people in her life.

"He asked me out," she said quietly. "But I don't think he wants Carolyn to know."

She saw Becki check the impulse to glance in Carolyn's direction. "Why not? She'd be thrilled."

"I don't know why not, but I'm going to find out tonight."

"Tonight? You're seeing him tonight?" Becki demanded, her voice an excited squeak.

Diana nodded. "I am so nervous. I don't know what to wear, how to act, what to say to him."

Becki patted her hand. "Just be yourself and he'll love you, just as everyone else does."

"He's not everyone else," she pointed out.

"No. I knew that when you told me you flirted with him."

Great. Everyone knew how she felt about him. His mother. Becki. Possibly Carolyn. Come to that, he probably knew too. She might as well make up a sign that said Diana Loves David and wear it around her neck.

"Diana! Come play with us!"

She glanced across the room where Carolyn was sitting, still watching her suspiciously. "We'll have to talk about this later," she said, getting to her feet. "Right now, I have some fences to mend."

She walked across the room and sank down on the carpet beside Carolyn and Susie. "Here, I am," she said brightly.

"Hi, Diana," Susie said, her blue eyes bright with welcome.

"Hi, honey," Diana said.

Carolyn watched with narrowed eyes, her lips pressed into an angry, thin line. "Why do you call everybody honey?"

"I like being called honey," Susie said, glaring at Carolyn. "Diana can call me honey anytime she wants."

"Oh, yeah?" Carolyn challenged. "Well, you're not really her honey." She turned to face Diana. "Tell her you like me best of all. Tell her!"

"No she doesn't like you best!" Susie said indignantly. "Why should she?"

"Because she likes my daddy! Not yours."

"She doesn't know my daddy!"

"Yeah? Well, she wouldn't like him even if she did because she likes mine!"

"No she doesn't!"

"Does too!"

Diana sighed. She should have seen this coming. "That's enough. Both of you. Who I like and don't like is not open for discussion. I like you both and I think you're both honeys," she said firmly.

Even as she spoke, she knew she was alienating Carolyn. But she couldn't admit to Susie that Carolyn was dearer to her than any of the other children.

"See! I told you!" Susie said triumphantly, snatched up her puzzle, and stormed away. Carolyn glared at her. "Why didn't you tell her the truth?"

"Because when you're here, I have to treat you just like the other children."

"Why can't you tell the truth?" she demanded, tears filling her eyes. "Don't you like me more?"

She stroked her hand against Carolyn's cheek, then bent her head to whisper in her ear. "Yes, I do."

"Then why didn't you say so?"

"Because I can't. Not here. Here I have to treat you all the same. But when we're away from here, I can show you how I feel. Do you understand?"

Carolyn looked mutinous for a moment, then she threw her arms around her neck and kissed her. "Okay. All right, as long as you're sure you like me more."

She hugged Carolyn to her. "Oh, honey, I do."

Chapter Nine

David and Mike stood on the scaffolding, looking down onto the construction site. "I think Jones is going to work out just fine on the crane, Dave."

He nodded and pushed his hard-hat further down on his head. "How are things going with you and Jill?" he asked.

"Great. She's the best thing that ever happened to me, man. I'm going to ask her to marry me."

He turned to look at Mike. "I didn't know you were that serious."

Mike nodded. "Oh, yeah, and I want her out of circulation."

"Do you ever...when you two first started dating, did you take her flowers?"

"What's this? You writing a book?" Mike asked, laughing.

"I just wondered...I have a date tonight and I'm a little out of practice. I'm not sure if I should take flowers."

Mike shrugged. "I guess it depends on how strong an impression you want to make. I knew the first time I saw Jill that I could really go for her. So I turned the big guns on her. Flowers, candy, dancing, phone calls in the middle of the day just to say hi. You know. The works."

"You knew the first time you saw her?"

Mike nodded. "Didn't you know when you saw Harriet?"

"No, but I knew I never wanted to date anyone else after I met her."

"And this woman you're seeing tonight? What about her? Who is she by the way?"

"She's one of the owners at Carolyn's daycare."

"The one your mom's been bugging you to take out?"

He turned back to watch the crane lifting several hundred pounds of dirt. "Yes. She seems like ... a nice lady."

"What's she like? Anything like Harriet?"

"No!" He swung around to look at Mike. "You think I'm looking for a substitute for her? Well, I'm not. I could never love another woman like I did her. Never."

Mike held up his hands. "Okay. Okay. It was just an innocent question. Don't go ballistic on me, man."

He let out a long breath and laughed self-consciously. "Sorry. I guess I'm a little uptight."

"A little, you say?"

"Okay, a lot."

"Why?"

"I like her. She's warm, attractive, funny, and she and Carolyn are crazy about each other."

"So what's she like?"

"That's the strange part, Mike. You know I like petite women of average height."

Mike, who at six-two, was only three inches shorter than David, grimaced. "Never understood that about you. Personally, I like a woman who has a little meat on her bones and is tall enough that I don't have to bend over double to kiss her. Makes her more huggable."

"Diana is very...huggable."

Mike's eyes widened. "You mean she's not about five-foot high and supermodel thin?"

"She's about five nine or ten and she definitely weighs more than a hundred pounds. She has beautiful dark skin."

"How dark?"

He shrugged. "Dark chocolate?"

Mike slapped him on the back. "A full-figured, black woman is the only way to go, man."

He laughed. "Don't be ridiculous."

Mike shrugged, looking smug. "Ridiculous? I barely heard a peep out of you when you went out with those other women your mom set you up with. But you start thinking romance when you meet a woman with pigment in her skin and meat on her bones? You want to know about flowers."

"Size has nothing to do with it. And neither does her skin color."

"I'm impressed. I didn't know you had such depth."

Diana studied her reflection in the full-length mirror on the back of one of her closet doors. She wore a light blue two-piece dress with short sleeves, a full skirt, and a matching jacket in a slightly darker shade.

Just before she left for a date of her own, Becki had assured Diana she would knock David's socks off. Now that she was alone, waiting for him, she wasn't so sure.

She glanced at her bedside clock. It was six-fifty. She'd find out what he thought in about ten minutes. She gave her face a final pat with her powder puff, slipped her feet into a pair of dark blue pumps, gathered her handbag, the shoe bag that held her walking shoes, and went into the living room to wait.

She was pacing the floor when the bell rang five minutes later. She went over to answer call box next to the apartment entrance door. "Yes?"

"Diana. Hi. It's David."

She glanced down at herself. "Did you want to come up?"

"Ah, no. I'll wait down here."

She took several deep breaths before slowly walking down the two flights of steps. At the front door, she took one final breath before opening the door.

"Hi." His gaze flicked quickly over her before he met her gaze. "You look nice."

Just nice? Not pretty or attractive or good enough to take his breath away? Apparently not. Nice was better than nothing.

She studied him. He wore a dark suit that emphasized the breadth of his shoulders. It fit so well it might have been made especially for him. She smiled. "You don't look so bad yourself."

For a moment, they stood staring at each other. About the time she noticed his right hand was behind his back, he bought it out and offered her a bouquet of white and yellow carnations. "I hope these are all right."

"Oh." She accepted them with a big smile. She inhaled their fragrance before speaking. "They're perfect. Thank you!" Impulsively, she leaned up and kissed his cheek.

He caught his breath and stepped away from her.

Her face flooded with heat. "I'm sorry!"

He shook his head. "No. I'm the one who needs to apologize." He reached behind her to close the door. "We should go. We have reservations."

She sighed. "I think this is a mistake, David."

He looked at her in surprise. "What is?"

"This date. Me. You. You're not ready to date."

"I am."

"Well if you are, I'm clearly not your type. No matter what I say or do, it seems to be the wrong thing. I'm not going out with you."

"Tonight?"

"Or any other night." She turned and reached for the doorknob. Surprise flooded through her when his big hand came down over hers, immobilizing it. "David, please. I know you don't really want to take me out."

"You don't know any such thing," he said, gently turning her to face him. "I do want to take you out."

"Why? Because Carolyn wants you to? Or because your mother does? Don't tell me you want to take me out and expect me to believe it."

His eyes narrowed. "That's exactly what I am telling you. And yes I do expect you to believe it, because it's the truth."

She studied his face in the light of the street lamp. He seemed sincere. Her heart beat quickened when he suddenly bent his head and brushed his lips against her cheek, close to, but not quite touching her mouth. "David..."

"Give me another chance. Please."

"No." She pushed against his shoulders.

He immediately stepped back. "Why not?"

If he didn't know, what was the point of trying to explain?

He closed his eyes briefly. "Please, Diana. I know I've been a bit of a klutz, or jerk if you prefer, but it's been a long time since I've been out with any...you're the only woman I've wanted to go out with since Harriet died."

When she remained silent, he reached out and took her hand in his. Holding her gaze with his, he brought her hand up to his lips.

She tingled all over as he brushed his lips against the back of her hand before planting a gentle kiss in her palm. *Oh, girl, keep it together. This man is going to hurt you if you don't.*

"You've filled my thoughts since we met. You are the only woman I've been attracted to since Harriet. Please bear with me?"

If she had half the sense she'd been born with, she'd tell him she had no interest or intentions of bearing with him. She nodded instead. *Oh, Diana, girl, what are you doing? He's going to break your heart.*

He pressed another kiss in her palm, linked his fingers with hers, and led her to his SUV.

She waited until he was seated beside her and had started the engine before she turned to look at him. "Have you talked to Carolyn today?"

"Yes. I talked to her just before I came to pick you up."

"Did you tell her where you were going?"

He replied after a noticeable pause. "No."

"Why not?"

He didn't look at her. "She's very impulsive."

"And?"

She saw his hands tighten on the steering wheel. "She'd expect us to come back from this date married. She wouldn't understand."

"What wouldn't she understand? That you're not ready to get serious?"

He maneuvered his vehicle onto the on ramp of Interstate 95 before he responded. "Are you?"

She looked out the window. There wasn't much to see except the tall abandoned factory buildings dotting the section of the city near the on-ramp. "Yes." She practically whispered the word.

When he didn't respond, she turned to find him staring straight ahead, his hands clenched on the steering wheel.

"I won't hurt you," he finally said.

"I'm counting on that, David."

Without taking his eyes off the road, he reached out a hand to squeeze hers.

She returned the pressure of his hand and felt some of the tension leave her body.

"I wish you would tell Carolyn. She was very upset with me today. She knew you called and thought I wouldn't let you talk to her."

He released her hand and placed his hand back to the steering wheel. "Fine. If you insist."

"I don't insist. I'm asking. I don't like her thinking she can't trust me."

"Okay. I'll tell her."

"Good. What about some music?"

"Help yourself," he said, sounding more relaxed.

She turned the radio on and the interior was filled with the soft, muted sounds of jazz. She sighed, relaxed back against her seat, and closed her eyes.

They made the rest of the drive in a comfortable silence. He parked the SUV in the restaurant parking lot, and they walked, hand in hand, into the restaurant. Diana felt as if she were floating, she was so happy. Granted they had a long way to go. They might not even make it, but she was satisfied with the way things were at the moment. The interior of the restaurant was dimly lit with high backed booths that created a romantic atmosphere. She slipped into the booth and looked up to find him watching her. She smiled. "This is nice."

"You like it? Good. I wasn't sure. A friend told me it was nice here."

So he hadn't brought his wife there. They could make their own memories. "It is." She picked up the menu. She was tempted to order a steak with all the trimmings. That way laid even more excess pounds. She couldn't afford to put on any more weight if she was going to keep him interested.

She ordered soup and a tossed salad. "No dessert," she told the waiter.

David looked at her in surprise. "That's it? Are you sure?"

She had to start sometime. Might as well be now. She nodded firmly. "Yes, thanks."

"Suit yourself." He turned to the waiter. "I'll have French Onion soup, followed by the New York Sirloin, well-done with a baked potato with butter."

"There! You see," she said, pointing a finger at him. "I knew you would do that!"

"Do what?"

"Order a steak after I've just ordered broth and a salad."

"Oh. I see," he said, nodding slowly, smiling. "You want to eat rabbit food, so I'm supposed to suffer with you. I don't think so. I work hard and I need my strength."

It was nice to see him really smile. She propped her elbows on the table, her chin on her hands and studied his face. "Tell me about David Jordan."

"Okay," he answered readily enough. "What would you like to know?"

"Everything. You see, I find him totally fascinating."

"Really? I hear he can be a real jerk sometimes."

She grinned. "Maybe so, but he's a charming one."

He laughed, but sobered quickly. "You're as kind as you are pretty."

She blushed, but didn't look away. "As long as you think so."

"I do," he said quietly, his blue gaze on her face.

"Now that we have that out of the way, I'm still waiting to hear about you."

"Well, there's not that much to tell."

"Tell me what there is to tell."

He took a sip of his iced tea. "I suppose you want to know about Harriet."

He wasn't smiling now and neither was she. "If it's not too painful."

"We met in college and started dating right away. We married right after graduation." He paused as the waiter brought her broth and his onion soup.

She tasted her broth, trying not to notice the heavenly aroma coming from his soup. "What was she like?"

"To look at?"

She nodded.

"She was slender, about five-five with long honey-blond hair and beautiful sea-green eyes like Carolyn's."

"She must have been beautiful."

"She was the most beautiful, sweetest person I ever met. She was warm, funny, understanding, the love of my life, and my best friend. But above all, she was a devout Christian."

Diana paused, choosing her next words carefully. "I understand she was killed by a drunken driver."

He nodded curtly and slipped his soup in silence.

"Having Carolyn must have been a great comfort to you."

It was the right thing to say. His smile returned. "I don't think I could have made it without her."

"She's very sweet."

"When she wants to be," he said, smiling. "You wouldn't believe how stubborn she can be." He pushed his soup bowl away and sat back against the booth. "That's enough about me. Tell me why you're not married."

She wanted to know so much more about him, but she readily followed his lead in changing the subject. "When I was fifteen, I decided I wanted to be a Christian in the biblical sense; doing the things God approved while avoiding those he didn't. I still want that. I'm not married because I haven't met a man who wants the same thing.

"Besides," she grinned at him. "I'm kind of out spoken."

His eyes twinkled with amusement. "So I've noticed."

"It turns a lot of men off."

"Not this one."

"Oh, good, because I seem to be even worse with you."

They stopped talking as the waiter approached to take away their soup bowls and replace them with their main course.

His steak emitted a heavenly aroma. Her nose twitched. Squaring her shoulders, she picked up her knife and fork. She tried not to notice as David began to cut his steak.

"So, tell me about your hobbies."

"What?" She stared at his steak. It looked so good she could almost taste it. And the potato was overflowing with butter. Her stomach grumbled in protest.

"Your hobbies," he prodded. "Tell me about them."

"What hobbies?"

His lips twitched, and he put down his knife and fork. "You've changed your mind about the salad? Would you like to share this steak?"

"Do you mind?" she asked.

He'd barely shaken his head before she was reaching for the plate. She resisted the urge to cut the steak into two equal portions and cut off a small piece instead. Then she eyed the potato. "Do you mind?"

He laughed, shaking his head. "You're shameless."

"I'm not," she protested, placing her baked roll on the table cloth to make room for the piece of steak and potato. "Well, maybe just a little. But only with you."

"I'm flattered."

"You should be!" she retorted and they both laughed.

"I'll call the waiter back and you can order a steak of your own."

She shook her head. "I don't want a steak."

"Then what's that on your saucer?"

"I'm watching my weight."

He met her gaze. "You don't need to worry about your weight, Diana. You...you're...you don't need to worry about your weight with me."

She smiled. "Thanks, but I don't want a steak."

He laughed.

They ended up sharing their meal. He cut another piece of steak for her and she gave him half of her salad.

By the time they left the restaurant to walk, hand in hand along the pier, Diana felt as if she'd known him all her life. And had loved him even longer. She was so happy. So thankful to the Lord for finally answering her prayer.

Chapter Ten

"You never told me what your hobbies were," David reminded her, as they stopped along the pier to gaze across the Delaware River to the New Jersey coast.

It was a warm night. They encountered several other couples on the pier at Penn's Landing. Some strolled hand in hand; others sat close with their feet hanging over the water far below.

Diana leaned on the railing several feet above the murky river. "I spend a lot of time involved in church activities. I'm a member of the choir and I try to visit the sick and shut-ins as often as I can. But I like walking, roller-skating, bowling, cooking, and reading British mysteries."

"Roller-skating is one of Carolyn's favorite pastimes."

"I know." She turned her head to find him staring at her. "Carolyn tells me you're an excellent skater."

"Oh, she does, does she?"

"Yes." She smiled. "You have no secrets from me."

He grinned. "I'll keep that in mind the next time I'm tempted to tell that lovable blabber mouth anything."

"What about you? What do you like to do? What do you read?"

"I don't get to do it much anymore, but I like playing basketball. I also like to fish. I lift weights and jog to help relieve tension and stress. When I have time, I like reading science fiction."

"When do you read?"

"Generally the only time I get to read is at lunch or while I'm fishing. Do you like fishing?"

"What kind?"

"Deep sea or just going out to Cobbs Creek Park?"

"I don't know. I've never tried it."

"Would you like to?"

She arched a brow at him. "Is that an invitation, David?"

"Yes."

She smiled. "I accept, if you'll do something with me."

"Okay. Shoot."

"Come to church with me some Sunday."

She felt him stiffen beside her. She touched his arm. "What's wrong?"

"Nothing. I just don't have much use for church lately."

Diana felt as if she'd been hit squarely in the pit of her stomach, knocking the wind out of her. He had to believe in God. "Why not?"

He looked away from her, back out onto the darkened horizon. "Harriet lay in a coma for two weeks fighting for her life. I spent almost every waking hour of that time praying, begging God to spare her life or to at least allow her to regain consciousness long enough for me and Carolyn to tell her one last time how much we loved her and to be able to say goodbye."

"And?"

"She died without regaining consciousness."

She stroked a hand down his arm. "I'm so sorry for you both, but do you blame God?"

He turned to stare at her. "I didn't say that. All I'm saying is up to that point I tried my best to be a decent, God-fearing man, and when I needed help, I didn't get any."

"Oh, David!" She slipped her arm through his and squeezed it against her side. "That must have been an awful time for you, but —"

He pulled away from her. "I don't want or need to be lectured, Diana. I get way too much of that from my mother. I'm not saying that I don't believe in God anymore. I'm just saying I need a little more time to...can you understand what I'm saying?"

"I don't know," she admitted. "I can't imagine not depending on my faith to get me through whatever life sends my way. It's how I coped when a drunk driver killed my parents. So you see, I'm not lecturing you. I understand how frustrated and angry you must feel, but—"

"What happened to the person responsible for your parents' death? Did this person at least go to prison?"

"Yes. He got five to ten years, but my parents are still dead, David. Just as your Harriet is."

"And I suppose you're going to tell me you don't feel any malice toward the driver or any loss of faith as a result?"

"I did feel malice, anger, and so many more emotions toward him. My parents were the anchor of our family. They were only in their fifties. There were so many more years ahead of them. I intended to pamper and shelter them when they were older. I envisioned protecting them as they'd always protected me. And when I got married and had kids, I expected them to pamper and spoil them.

"A large part of my future happiness was wrapped up in my parents. Then, suddenly, they were both snatched from my life. I had to pray long and hard not to hate the man who took them from me."

"Didn't he deserve your hatred?"

"Hating him would have taken an emotional and spiritual toil on me. Even if I'd allowed myself to hate him, my parents were still going to be dead. My faith got me through those dark days and weeks after their death."

"You faith was never shaken?"

She shook her head. "I'm not saying I've always done the right thing because I haven't. However, I do my best and I know that sometimes bad things happen to good people. But that doesn't mean that God doesn't love or care about me...about us...about you, David."

"How can you be so sure that's not exactly what it means?"

She shook her head. "I decided to look upon my parents' death as a challenge to my faith that I was determined to meet and conquer. I threw all my anger and animosity on God and as he's always done, he sustained me. Now my faith is stronger than ever. I've seen first-hand how good He and my faith can be and I know they will both sustain me no matter what happens in life."

"I'm obviously not as forgiving as you are. Nor is my faith as strong. I'm not so sure there's any reward for being a dutiful Christian."

"David, if you'd only go to God and pray—"

"I'm not interested in doing that just now," he cut her off quickly.

"Oh...David..."

He stared at her. "Is that going to be a problem for you?"

"I...oh, David, I..."

He sighed. "I take it that's a yes."

His voice sounded so bleak, she slipped her arm through his again. "Will you think about coming to church with me? I'd like you to hear me sing in the choir. Sometimes, I do a solo. We have a concert coming up in about six weeks. I'd love for you to come hear us sing."

He looked down at her. "I would love to hear you sing and I would like to go on seeing you, Diana."

"But?"

"No buts. I want to see you again. However, I do need you to understand the current state of my...faith."

"Is that a no? You won't come?"

"No." He shook his head. "It's not a no. I'll come. Just don't ask me to come this week."

"Okay. What about the week after or the one after that?"

He laughed. "You don't give up, do you?"

"Not when the cause is worthwhile."

"And you think I am?"

She placed a hand against his chest and smiled up at him. "Oh, yes, David. I do."

He lifted her hand to brush his lips against her fingers. "I hope you never have cause to change your mind."

"I don't think I ever will. I'm not fickle, David. I know how I feel and what I want out of life." She bit back the urge to say she wanted him. She had a feeling he already knew that.

He bent his head to touch his mouth against hers.

She closed her eyes.

He pressed a soft, sweet kiss against her lips.

She resisted the urge to run her fingers through his hair, but leaned against him.

He slipped his arm around her waist and kissed her again.

She parted her lips, enjoying and welcoming the longer, warmer kiss. When he clasped a hand on the back of her neck and she felt his tongue touching hers, she pressed a hand against his shoulder. "David..."

He nibbled at her mouth. "What?"

"I think we should stop."

His arm tightened against her waist. "I'm just getting warmed up."

"I don't want you to get too warm."

He laughed, but lifted his head. "Diana—"

She moistened her lips. "Will you come to see me sing?"

"There's a good chance I wouldn't go before or after, but I will come to see you sing."

It was a start. "I'll hold you to that."

He laughed. "I'm sure you will." He bent his head.

She sucked in a quick breath before she leaned into him with her lips parted.

He kissed her again. He did it so quickly she barely had time to respond before he was lifting his head. "It's getting late. We'd better head back."

She nodded. Standing in the moonlight trading kisses was a recipe for disaster.

They walked back to his SUV and he held the passenger door open for her.

When they were both inside with their seatbelts on, he started the engine and drove away. "Do you have any brothers or sisters, Diana?"

"No. I'm an only child."

"That must have made losing both parents in the same accident even worse."

"It did, which is why I had to rely so heavily on my faith. What about you, David? Do you have any siblings?"

"No."

They made the rest of the drive to her apartment in silence. Diana spent the time in silent prayer. She had her work cut out for her, trying to get him back on track with God. Still, she had a feeling he would be worth any amount of effort she expended on his behalf. And God must have brought them together for a reason.

"I enjoyed tonight, David," she said as they stood together at her door. "Thank you for asking me out."

He caressed her cheek. "I enjoyed it too. Thank you for coming."

The urge to lean into him and part her lips for a kiss was difficult to resist. "You'll tell Carolyn about tonight?"

"Yes, I'll tell her." He lifted her hand to his mouth and kissed her palm several times.

Her heart raced and she longed to have him take her in his arms and kiss her breathless. "Well...good night."

He touched his lips to her fingertips. "Good night."

She moistened her lips and looked up at him. "David..."

"Yes?" He raised his gaze from her hands to look at her mouth.

"Are you going to just stand here holding my hand and staring at me all night or are you going to kiss me goodnight?"

He released her hand and cupped her face in his big, warm palms. "I am definitely going to kiss you," he breathed the words against her mouth.

Even as she told herself she shouldn't, she parted her lips.

He brushed his lips against hers.

Her stomach muscles clenched. "David..."

He slipped his arms around her before he settled his mouth on hers.

Unable to resist the temptation, she slipped her arms around his neck.

He swept the tip of his tongue against her lips before he tightened his arms around her. The kisses that followed were longer, warmer, and filled her with improper desires.

Afraid of the emotions he was arousing, she gasped and pushed against his shoulders.

He resisted for several moments before he finally dragged his mouth away from her.

She pushed against his shoulders again.

He dropped his arms around her waist, but caught one of his hands in hers.

She tugged at her hand. "I...I...I'd better go in."

He nodded silently, but continued to hold her hand again.

She tugged at her hand. "David..."

He sighed and released it with obvious reluctance.

Her heart beat like a drum and she felt hot and filled with desire. "So I'm going inside now before things get too heated."

"They're already heated.

"David..."

He shrugged and stepped away from her. "So go."

She went.

David watched Diana go inside and waited until he heard the locks clicking before he turned and walked back to his SUV. Inside, he sat taking slow deep breaths for a minute before he started the engine and drove to his mother's house.

She answered the door wearing a robe. "David! Is something wrong, dear?"

"No. Did I wake you?"

"No. I was just sitting in the living room reading the Bible."

"I didn't mean to disturb you and I know Carolyn's probably asleep, but I want to talk to her."

"Come in, dear, come in." She stepped away from the door.

He walked inside.

She leaned against the closed door and studied his face. "So? You look...content. How did your date with Diana go?"

He grinned. "It went, Mom."

She smiled. "Yes?"

He nodded. "Yes. I think ..."

"Yes, dear?"

The expectant look on her face snapped him back to his senses. He was too old to allow a few kisses, no matter how heated, to cause him to lose his prospective. "I like her," he said simply. It was too early to say or even think any further than that.

She nodded, looking smug. "I thought you would, dear."

He leaned down and kissed her cheek. "Thank you."

"For what?"

"For inviting her to dinner on Sunday without telling me."

"Would you have come if I'd told you?"

"No." He shrugged. "I don't know. I might have come."

"Why?"

"I've thought about her a lot since we met. I..."

"What is it, dear. What bothers you about her? Her size?" she probed gently.

He shook his head. "Her size is not an issue. It never really was."

She bit her lip. "I didn't raise you in a manner that would make her skin color important."

"And I never said it was. As a matter of fact, I find her skin tone charming."

She sighed in relief. "So?"

He shrugged. "She's not like anyone I've ever met before. She's amazing and I..."

"Oh, David!" She hugged him and kissed his cheek. "You're going to see her again."

He nodded slowly. "I suppose now I'll never hear the end of mother knows best."

She smiled.

He glanced over his shoulder toward the staircase. "I'm going up to see Carolyn."

"Good idea, dear."

He ran up the stairs and went down the hall to the middle bedroom. The door was open and a night light cast a muted glow onto the bed and the small child lying there.

He sat on the side of the bed and lifted Carolyn gently into his arms. "Carolyn? Sweetie?"

She yawned, opened her eyes, and threw her arms around his neck. "Daddy! I was just dreaming about you. Hoping you'd come for me and here you are!"

"It's after ten. That's too late to get you out of bed and take you home. I just wanted to explain who I was with tonight."

She pulled away and stared into his eyes. "Daddy? Oh, Daddy! Were you with...Diana?"

He nodded. "Yes. We had dinner. I'm sorry I didn't tell you earlier."

"I was hurt because you said we had to be straight up with each other."

"I know and I'm sorry."

She flashed him a sunny smile. "That's okay, Daddy. Did you like her? Did you kiss her goodnight? Are you going to take her out again? Are you —"

He laughed. "Hey, hey, hey. Not so fast with the questions. Yes, I like her."

"How much?"

"A lot," he admitted. "And yes I am going to take her out again."

"Yes!" Carolyn pumped a small, clenched fist in elation. "Yes!"

He laughed and kissed her cheek. "Now I'm going to let you get back to sleep and I'll see you tomorrow after work."

"But Daddy! You didn't tell me if you kissed her. Did you?"

He laid her on the bed and gently tapped the tip of her nose. "That's none of your business, Sweetcakes. One more thing. When I called the daycare earlier, I should have asked to speak to you. That was an oversight on my part and not Diana's fault. Okay?"

Carolyn frowned. "She told on me? She's a blabbermouth tattletale!"

"She didn't tell on you. And you watch your tongue, young lady," he reprimanded her. "She was upset that you were angry with her. She's very fond of you."

"I know that, Daddy," she said meekly.

"Good. So you're not angry with her. Right?"

"Right, Daddy." She grinned at him. "I knew you'd like Diana, Daddy," she said happily.

"Well, you were right." He kissed her and drew the covers back up to her neck.

"Are you going to marry Diana, Daddy?"

He suppressed a groan and chose his words carefully. "I've only gone out with her once."

"But you already know you like her."

"Yes, but when a man and woman get married, it's because they love each other very much and want to spend the rest of their lives together."

"I know that," she said indignantly. "So are you going to marry her? Is she going to be my new Mommy?"

"Carolyn, honey, I need you to understand that it's too early in our relationship to even think about marriage."

"Oh. Well, I'll bet you do marry her, Daddy."

"Carolyn—"

"You said you weren't taking her out and you did, so maybe you'll marry her."

"Don't count on that, young lady," he said firmly.

"Okay, Daddy." She gave him a confident smile.

He sighed. Why had he allowed Diana to talk him into telling Carolyn about their date? Now it would be nearly impossible to convince her that he wasn't going to marry Diana.

"It's time for you to get back to sleep."

"Okay, Daddy. Thank you for coming to tell me."

He kissed her. "I'll see you tomorrow night. I love you."

"I love you too, Daddy. And so does Diana."

He left the room quickly before Carolyn could ask if he loved Diana.

At home, he undressed, got in bed, turned out the lights, and picked up the phone. He dialed, then smiled when he heard Diana's voice. "Hi."

"David."

He liked the way her voice softened as she said his name. "I know it's late and I won't keep you. I just wanted to thank you for having dinner with me."

"It was my pleasure."

"Mine as well. I also wanted to ask if we could see you Saturday."

"We? As in you and George Clooney?"

He laughed. "He probably has other plans. Will you settle for me and Carolyn?"

"In a heartbeat."

"Good. I stopped by my mother's and told Carolyn about us."

"Oh." She sounded pleased. "Is there an us, David?"

"There will be if I have anything to say about it."

"Then here's hoping you have plenty to say about it."

He laughed. "Oh, Diana. I like you."

"I like you."

"I like you a lot, Diana."

"Same here."

He sighed. "I know I'm not easy to know, but I hope you can bear with me."

"We'll see."

"What about Saturday? Do we have a date?"

"Why don't you and Carolyn come here for dinner around six? I'll prepare a special meal."

"What?"

"Come and find out."

"All right. We'll see you Saturday at six."

Chapter Eleven

"I thought you'd be happy for me, Becki."

Diana watched as Becki looked up from the desk in the daycare center early the next morning. She and Becki were the only ones in the room. Diana sat in a large chair pulled up to the other side of the desk. The first child wasn't due to arrive for another half hour, and the staff had not yet arrived.

Becki shook her head. "Oh, come on. Don't look at me like that. I am happy for you!"

"Oh?"

"Well. Okay. I *would* be happy for you if things were different."

Diana frowned. "Different how?"

"Well, you said yourself that you couldn't change anyone and that you couldn't date a man who didn't have a strong faith. Doesn't that sort of leave David Jordan out of the picture?"

"No! He has faith," Diana objected. "He just needs a little help rechanneling."

"And you're going to give him that help?"

"Yes, I am."

"What if he doesn't respond? What if he ends up weakening your faith?"

133

"That is not going to happen, Becki," she said curtly.

"Yeah? Well, you know what the scriptures say about he who thinks he's standing being aware he doesn't fall."

"What? Where'd you hear that?"

Becki arched a brow. "I read it in the Bible. The apostle Paul wrote it at first Corinthians 10:12."

"I know the scripture," she said wearily.

Becki nodded knowingly. "You just didn't think I did? Well, I've been reacquainting myself with the Bible. So brace yourself."

"Why?"

"Now, that's a strange question coming from you, Diana."

"Oh, I didn't mean it like that," she said quickly. "I think it's great you're reading the Bible again. I just meant are you doing it for yourself or because it's what Paul wants you to do?"

"At first it was just to please Paul," she admitted. "but the more I read the Bible, the more I realize how much I don't know. Then I realized I wanted to know more for myself."

"I'm really pleased, Becki, and I hope things work out for you and Paul. I just wished you were pleased for me. I wish you'd pray for me and David."

"I will. I just wish..."

"What?"

"He sounds as if he needs a lot of work. He sounds so bitter."

"He's not, bitter, Becki."

"Oh?"

She sighed. "Not really...but even if he were, he'd have a right to be," she said defensively.

"He has no more right than you do and you're not bitter."

"I loved my parents more than I can say, but I knew I'd lose them one day." She leaned forward, anxious to explain. "It's different for him. He expected to share the rest of his life with his wife. He lost more than I did, but I know he's a good man who just needs someone to help him rediscover his faith. And I'm that someone."

Becki smiled suddenly. "Hey, I'm a believer. I think you can accomplish just about anything you set your mind to."

"God willing," she said softly.

"And I'm thinking He is." Becki grinned. "So?"

"So what?"

"So did he kiss you?"

Diana felt her cheeks heating up. "I don't kiss and tell."

"So he did kiss you!" Becki grinned. "How was it? Did you see stars? Hear bells? Did your toes curl? What? Details, I need details."

Diana covered her hot cheeks with her hands. "Becki Howard, you're worse than Carolyn! I said I'm not telling."

"No?" She shrugged. "Well, you don't have to. You were practically floating around this morning. I think it's safe to assume he kissed you, all right. And I'm thinking your toes did curl, big time."

Diana made a zipping motion with her fingers. "I'll never tell."

"You already have." Becki grinned.

Two days later, David sat in his office at the townhouse construction site, his chair tilted back against the wall behind him, his feet propped up on the desk.

Mike sat in the only chair on the other side of the desk. "Earth to Dave. Earth to Dave."

He blinked and pulled his feet off the desk and sat up in his chair. "What?"

"You haven't heard a word I said."

"That's not true. You said something about the carpenters going out on strike next week. And that will just about shut down the entire job. We'll need to get as much done as possible between now and then." He ran a hand through his hair. "Between that and the shoddy materials the owners are trying to get past the city inspectors, you know there's going to be no bonus from this job."

Mike nodded. "Yeah and I was planning to use my share for a honeymoon."

"You've proposed to Jill already?"

"We're spending the weekend at her parents place in the Pocono Mountains. I'm going to pop the question then."

"With or without her parents?"

Mike frowned. "Definitely with. Jill's the old-fashioned type."

"Proposing is a big step."

Mike shook his head. "Not when you're in love, and I am. Surely you can understand that."

"What? Why do you say that?"

He shrugged. "In between staring off into space with a goofy look on your face, you look happy. Happier than I've seen you since Harriet was killed. This Diana of yours must be quite a lady."

David nodded. "Yes. She is, but we've only had one date, Mike."

"That must have been some date. Besides, sometimes it only takes one date or even one look to know you're with someone special."

"I didn't say—"

"Let's cut the crap, Dave. You're not interested in meeting anyone else. Are you?"

"No, but—"

"Can you see yourself with her for the rest of your life?"

He cast a quick glance at the picture of Harriet on his desk next to the phone. "I expected to spend my life with Harriet."

"I know. But she's dead, Dave. You and Carolyn are alive. Diana's alive. What you're feeling for her is good for all three of you."

He sighed, running his hand through his hair. "I guess."

"Of course it is." Mike glanced at his watch and rose. "Time to get back to the grind."

He nodded, waited until Mike had closed the door of the trailer, and then reached for the phone. He punched out Diana's number.

"Good morning, Happy Time Daycare. Becki Howard speaking."

"Ah, hi. May I speak to Miss Stuart?"

"May I ask who's calling?"

She would ask. "David Jordan," he said reluctantly.

"Oh, David. Hello."

"Hi."

"Hold on a second." A moment later, he heard Diana's voice on the line. "Hi, David."

"Hi. How are you?"

"I'm fine. Even better now that you've called."

He smiled. "You're amazing."

"Hmmm. I'm not sure if that's a compliment or not," she teased.

"It is. I find your honesty refreshing."

"Is that a good thing?"

138

"I think so. I've never met a woman so willing to speak so honestly about her feelings."

"Then I'm complimented."

"Good."

"Now what can I do for you?"

"I'm calling because..."

"Yes?"

"I didn't really want anything."

"No?" she sounded pleased. "You're calling to tell me you're thinking of me?"

"Yes," he said, admitted. "Are you a mind reader?"

"Don't I wish. Then I'd know what you were thinking and feeling when we're together."

"I was thinking about you so I called."

"Really? How sweet."

He lowered his voice. "I can be very sweet." He was amazed at how easy it was to flirt with her.

"Yeah? Well, I'll be the judge of that."

"I know we're going to see you on Saturday, but I was wondering if maybe Carolyn and I could stop over to see you tonight. We could have pizza or something."

"I'd love that, David, but it's Wednesday."

"And what? You don't eat on Wednesday?"

She laughed.

He smiled. He like the sound of her laughter and the way it filled him with hope.

"Very cute, Mr. Jordan."

"What's the but?"

"I have choir practice tonight. Of course, you and Carolyn are welcome to join me."

He studied the dull, beige wall of the trailer interior. "Ah, I don't think so."

"Why not, David?"

"We've already discussed why not, Diana."

"I know, but I wish you'd reconsider."

"We have a deal. Let's stick to it for now."

"Okay. For now."

"What time will you be finished practice? Could we see you then?"

"That won't be until around nine."

"That's too late for Carolyn on a school night."

"I'm sorry."

"So am I. I'd really like to see you before Saturday. What about lunch?" he suggested.

"Lunch? I'd love to have lunch with you. When?"

"I can't make it today. What about tomorrow? Do you take lunch away from the daycare?"

"I usually don't, but I can."

"How long do you have?"

"I can get Becki to cover for me for about an hour and a half or so."

"Do you drink?"

"Yes."

"Then how about we meet at the Tacony Street entrance of Tacony Creek Park around twelve? I won't be dressed for any place else. I hope you won't mind."

"No. I'll bring lunch."

"Good, but no rabbit food, please."

"For me or you?"

"For either of us," he said, laughing. "I might not be so inclined to share all my meals with you, you know."

He heard her sigh. "Some of us have to watch our weight."

"Why?"

"David, I'm aware of your preference for small, slender women. There's not much I can do about my height, but—"

"I thought I'd already made it clear I find you attractive just as you are."

"Oh, David! If only you meant that."

He sat forward in his seat, frowning. "I do mean it, Diana. I usually say exactly what I mean. How many ways do I need to say I don't have any issue with your height, your skin tone, your weight, or anything else about you?"

"I...thank you."

"So please, no rabbit food."

"Okay."

"Okay," he echoed, aware of an excitement at the thought of seeing her in just over twenty-four hours. "I'll see you tomorrow."

Diana paced up and down the sidewalk in front of the Tacony Street entrance to the park. Yet another glance at her watch revealed that it was now nearly twelve-thirty. Where was David? If she hadn't been so eager to see him, she might have remembered to pick up her cell phone from her desk before she left to meet him.

She'd give him five more minutes. Then she'd have to admit that she'd been stood up. She glanced down at the silk warm-up suit she was wearing. Why had she let Becki talk her into wearing it just so he could leave her standing in the middle of the sidewalk?

It would be a cold day in August before she agreed to go out with David Jordan again. He'd clearly had second thoughts and didn't even have the decency to cancel their date. She snatched up the insulated bag holding the lunch she'd packed and started down the sidewalk.

"Diana! Wait!"

She swung around to find David running toward her from the opposite direction. He wore jeans and a flannel shirt. He stopped just in front of her, looking harried.

"You're late," she said coolly. "Where have you been? I thought you weren't coming."

"I'm sorry. There was a problem on the site I had to handle before I left. I called the daycare, but you'd already left so I drove over to tell you in person."

"To tell me what?"

"That I can't make lunch."

"You mean you can't stay? You have to go back?"

He nodded. "Yes."

"Now? Don't you even have time for a sandwich?"

"I'm sorry, no."

After all the changes she'd made in her schedule to accommodate him? She made no effort to hide her exasperation. "Fine. Go back, David."

"Hey, come on," he said. "It's not as if I want to go back. I shouldn't even be here now, but I couldn't just leave you here waiting for me."

"Why not?" she demanded angrily. She didn't care if she was being reasonable or not. "You left me here for twenty minutes already. What would another hour be between friends?"

His eyes narrowed. "That couldn't be helped. You're not being fair."

"And you think you are? I'm supposed to just jump every time you call and then be understanding when you leave me standing in the middle of the sidewalk like a fool?"

His lips tightened into a thin line. "Yes, I did expect you to understand, but obviously that was expecting too much."

"Way too much, David."

He shook his head. "I don't have time for this, Diana."

"What? So now I'm wasting your time?" He narrowed his gaze. "Look. You can blow off steam later, but right now, I have to go."

"Then go. Just don't expect me to be waiting around the next time you feel like calling."

"If you can't understand I manage a construction site and have to be on hand to handle problems, then maybe you shouldn't expect me to feel like calling you again!" he retorted and stormed away.

Tears filled her eyes. She angrily blinked them away and spun on her heel. She walked in the opposite direction from the one he'd taken. By the time she'd reach her car, she hoped she'd vanquished the urge to cry.

She was several yards from the entrance where she'd left her car when she heard running footsteps behind her. Before she could turn, she felt a hand fall on her shoulder. "Diana..."

She pulled away and turned to face David. "What?"

"Look, Diana," he said in a low, angry voice. "You know you're not being fair. If I didn't have to go, I wouldn't. Please don't behave like some..." he trailed off, seemingly at a lost for the right word.

"Like some, what, David? Like some big blimp?"

He narrowed his gaze. "You know, you'd drive a saint to foul language."

"Since you're hardly a saint, what's your point?"

"I've never given you any reason to suggest I considered you...I've never given you any reason to say what you just did."

She swallowed hard. "Okay, maybe you didn't actually say anything, but I saw the surprise on your face when we first met."

He gripped her shoulders. "Whatever you think I might have thought when we met, you have to know that I am attracted to you now."

"I don't know any such thing." She turned away.

He caught her hand and turned her back to face him. "Yes, you do!"

She shook her head.

"Get a grip, Diana. If I weren't attracted to you, I wouldn't have asked you out the first time. Nor would I be here today." He drew her close and put his arms around her.

All desire to resist vanished. She leaned against him.

He tightened his arms around her and brushed his lips against her forehead.

Diana placed her hands on his shoulders and closed her eyes. Finally, she was where she most wanted to be—in his arms with his heart beating in sync with hers. She rubbed her cheek against his shoulder.

"I would have been here on time if I could. And I'd gladly stay if I could. Believe me."

Was it wise to believe him?

"Diana?"

She opened her eyes and lifted her head.

He bent his head, pausing with his lips a breath away from hers.

She parted her lips.

He pressed his mouth against hers in a warm kiss that removed any doubts she had about his finding her attractive.

"David," she brushed her fingers against his neck.

"Diana," he whispered her name and pressed a sweet, but gentle kiss against her mouth.

Only the fact that they were in the park kept her from linking her arms around his neck and inviting him to kiss her yet again. And not so gently this time.

All too quickly, he lifted his head and released her. "If I don't go, I'm going to have to go back to being a full-time accountant because I'll probably get fired." He stroked her cheek. "You wouldn't like me if I had to spend all day cooped up in some office crunching numbers."

"No?" She smiled up at him, resting her palms against his chest. "Who says I like you now?"

His eyes twinkled. "A little birdie told me you did."

"This little birdie wouldn't happen to be named Carolyn, would she?"

He laughed. "I don't gossip and tell."

"Oh, David! You're..."

"What?" he asked softly, staring down into her eyes. "Warm? Funny? Handsome? Irresistible?"

"Yes."

"Yes, I'm which one?"

"All of the above," she admitted.

His eyes gleamed with satisfaction. "We'll have to discuss how wonderful I am another time. Right now I need you to do us both a favor, honey. Let me go."

Honey. Hugging the endearment to her like a treasure, she nodded. "Then go."

He studied her face. "And you're no longer angry?"

"What I am is sorry. I let my disappointment make me unreasonable. I wanted to be with you."

He brushed his fingers against her lips. "I wanted that too. I thought about being with you all morning, but I really have to get back to the site."

The look in his eyes made her catch her breath. She smiled suddenly. "Go. I'm all right."

"I'll call you later."

"I'll be waiting."

He linked his fingers through hers and leaned down to reward her with a quick kiss.

She smiled and watched him until he disappeared around a bend in the park trail. Only then did she head back to her car. She changed her mind halfway there. She still had another forty minutes or so before she had to be back at the daycare. She went back into the park to sit on one of the benches. Thinking about David and the kisses they'd shared, she ate a ham sandwich on wheat, an apple, and drank a cherry soda.

She took the long way back to the daycare. A vase with Orchids, hibiscus, and red carnations sat on her desk.

"Guess who sent them," Becki whispered.

With a thumping heart, Diana lifted the card from the center of the flowers.

You're perfect — just the way you are. Can't wait to see you again. David.

She smiled. "I think he likes me after all, Becki."

Becki grinned. "I think that's a safe assumption."

Chapter Twelve

"Daddy! Daddy! Did you hear that?"

David lowered the evening paper, sat up in his recliner, and looked across his living room. Carolyn sat on the carpet in front of the television. They'd finished dinner half an hour earlier. Now they were relaxing before Carolyn had to go to bed.

"Hear what?"

"The carnival's in town, Daddy! Starting tomorrow. Can we go, Daddy? Can we? Please?"

"Where is it?"

"The lot behind the mall, Daddy. Can we go?"

"Sure. We'll go on Sunday afternoon."

Carolyn leapt to her feet and rushed across the room to climb onto his lap. "Oh, no, Daddy! Let's go tomorrow night."

"Sweetie, I was planning to ask Diana out tomorrow night."

"So? She can come with us!"

That wasn't exactly what he'd had in mind. He didn't want to risk having Carolyn think he didn't want her along. Besides, he really didn't care where he went or what he did, as long as he did it with Diana. "Okay. I'll ask her."

"Oh, good!" Carolyn covered his cheek with kisses.

"But if she doesn't want to go, you and I will go on Sunday. Okay?"

"Oh, she'll want to go," she said confidently. "She likes being with us. And we like being with her." She pulled back to look up at him. "Don't we, Daddy?"

"Yes, we do."

He called Diana after Carolyn was in bed. "I'm sorry about lunch today."

"So am I," she said, "but there will be other lunches."

"Oh, yes," he said.

"Then it's all right. Did you get the problems at work straightened out?"

"No. It's a mess," he said and found himself telling her about the slowdown of the carpenters that was almost certain to lead into a full-fledged strike during the following week.

She listened quietly, asking an occasional question that let him know she really was listening. Much like Harriet had done.

Only she wasn't Harriet. He stopped in mid-sentence.

"Go on," she urged. "I'm listening."

"I know you are, but I don't want to bore you."

"You're not boring me, David."

"That's nice to know, but that's enough about my job. I want to talk about you."

"Smart guy."

He laughed. "Tell me again why you've never been married."

"I thought I was close once."

"When was this? What happened?"

"About four years ago. He was funny, nice to be with, and we got along great. After a couple of months, he proposed."

He felt uncomfortable at the thought of Diana in love with another man. "And you said?"

"I said no when I found out he didn't want any kids. Not even one. I couldn't marry a man who didn't want kids."

"Did you love him?"

"At the time I thought I did," she said quietly. "Now I know the difference."

"Between?"

"Infatuation and the real thing."

His heartbeat quickened and he stifled the urge to pursue that line of questioning. He stretched out on his bed, his face turned away from Harriet's picture on his night stand. "And since then?"

"I've been waiting to meet someone who I could love who would want at least two kids. I think an only child leads a lonely existence." He heard her catch her breath. "Not that I'm criticizing you for having only one," she said quickly.

"Harriet and I never intended for Carolyn to be an only child. We just wanted to have a few years between kids so each child would have a chance to enjoy being the baby of the family."

"So you do want more children when you marry again?"

She sounded almost relieved, which somehow annoyed him. "Did I say I was going to remarry?"

"No, but I was sort of hoping that now you might want to."

He swallowed hard. There was only one way to interpret her remark. Things were spinning too fast.

"I'm sorry," she said when he didn't reply. "You probably think I'm the most shameless woman you've ever met."

While her frankness still occasionally unnerved him, he was flattered that it only happened with him.

"What I think is that I'd like to see you as often as possible," he said. He smiled when he heard her relieved laughter.

"Oh, David, I do try to exercise a little decorum with you, but..."

"Don't sweat it. I like you just the way you are."

"David." Her voice was husky. "I guess you know that I—"

"Like me too?" he asked quickly, interrupting her. He suspected she'd been about to say she loved him and he wasn't ready to hear such an admission for her—yet.

He heard the disappointment in her voice when she spoke again. "Yeah. I like you too."

"Ah, it's getting late. I need to hit the sack, but Carolyn wanted me to ask if you'd like to come to the carnival behind the mall with us tomorrow night."

"Carolyn wanted you to ask?"

"I put that badly. She's the one who wants to go to the carnival. But I'd hoped to ask you out to dinner."

"I haven't been to a carnival in years. I'd love to go."

"Great. Carolyn and I will pick you up around six-thirty. I thought maybe we could stop for pizza on the way."

"Okay. Good night."

"Good night, Diana."

After he hung up, he continued lying on the bed, this time staring at Harriet's picture. It felt strange to feel so excited and energized by the thought of seeing a woman other than Harriet. He hadn't expected to want another woman so much.

It was no use thinking he wasn't ready to get serious with Diana. He spent most of his time away from her thinking about her and trying to figure when he'd see her next. When he looked down into her warm, brown gaze or held her in his arms and kissed her, he felt whole. Complete. Happy. But part of him knew it was indecent to feel this way so soon. Harriet had been dead for less than two years, and already he was longing to be with another woman.

The carnival was in full swing by the time Diana, David, and Carolyn arrived.

"Oh, Daddy! I'm so excited. I don't know what to do first!" Carolyn exclaimed, her eyes filled with wonder as she glanced around at all the rides. She stood between Diana and David, a hand in each one of theirs. She squeezed Diana's. "Isn't this nice, Diana?"

It wasn't as nice as Diana had expected it to be. She'd been looking forward to being with David and Carolyn, but she'd noticed a coolness in David's manner the moment she saw him. She smiled down at Carolyn. "It's very nice, honey."

"It's nice being with Daddy and me, isn't it?"

"Yes." She glanced up to find David watching her. She flashed him a quick smile and looked away.

"What ride would you like to get on first, sweetie?" He asked Carolyn.

"Can we all get on them together, Daddy?"

Diana felt his gaze on her, but she didn't look at him. "If Diana wants too, we can."

Carolyn tugged at her hand. "Do you want to?"

She didn't. She smiled down at Carolyn. "I think it'll be more fun if we take turns, don't you?"

"What do you mean?" Carolyn asked, frowning.

"Well, some rides you'll get on with your dad and some with me. Okay?"

"Don't you want to get on with me and Daddy?"

"No," she said, smiling to take the sting out of her confession. "This way will be more fun."

"Okay. I'll go with Daddy first. Okay?"

She nodded, still not looking at David. "Okay, honey."

She and David took turns getting on rides with Carolyn, which meant that they spent very little time in each other's company. Which, she sensed was the way he wanted it. She suspected his lack of warmth was a direct result of her practically proposing to him the night before. Now he was probably afraid to say or do anything she might misconstrue.

They'd been at the carnival for an hour when Diana saw Becki in the company of a tall, attractive male.

"Hi, Becki!" Carolyn said happily.

"Hi Carolyn."

"Becki! This is a surprise." Diana turned to face the man standing next to Becki. "You must be Paul Hamilton Mitchell."

He looked surprised. "Have we met?"

"Oh, no, it's just that Becki talks about you so much that I feel like we have."

"Hey, girl, zip it up!" Becki protested.

Diana widened her eyes. "You didn't want him to know?" She asked sweetly. "Sorry." She turned to David. "This is David Jordan, who already knows how frequently I think of him."

After the two men had shaken hands, Becki looked down at Carolyn. "Having a good time, sweetie?"

"I'm having a great time! Are you?"

"We would, if we only had someone like you to tell us which rides are the best. I'm thinking you know the best ones."

Carolyn nodded happily and Diana stared at Becki, wondering what she was up to.

Becki looked at David. "I wonder if you'd mind if Paul and I borrowed Carolyn for awhile?"

He looked down at Carolyn. "Honey, what do you think? Do you want to go?"

"Won't you miss me if I do, Daddy?"

"Of course I will," he answered promptly. "But I have you all the time. It's okay with me if you want to go."

"We really need to borrow you," Becki said.

Carolyn giggled and looked up at Diana. "I'm very popular, Diana."

"Of course you are, honey."

"Okay." Carolyn pulled her hand from Diana's and offered it to Becki. "You can borrow me for awhile."

"Oh, thanks, sweetie," she said, taking Carolyn's hand. Her gaze encompassed both Diana and David. "Shall we meet at the ticket booth in an hour and a half?"

David nodded.

Diana watched the trio walk away with a feeling of trepidation. Being left alone with David in his present mood was the last thing she wanted.

"Which ride would you like to try next?" he asked her, his gaze on the big Ferris Wheel off to their left.

"Actually, I don't want to get on any."

He brought his gaze back to her face. "Tired?"

"No. I just don't like carnival rides." She looked down at her sneakers, sunk at least half an inch in mud. Fortunately her sneaks were disposable. "Or carnivals."

He frowned. "Then why did you come?"

"Because I wanted to be with you and Carolyn," she said slowly and sighed when he looked away from her.

Great. She'd scared him off with her honesty.

"How do you suggest we spend the next ninety minutes, Diana?"

"You could take me home and be back here before Carolyn knew you were gone."

"Take you home? Don't you feel well?"

"I'm fine, but I'd like to go home."

"Why?"

"Does it matter why?" she asked, hoping it would matter to him.

He shook his head and shrugged. "No, I guess not."

"Good. Then take me home."

"Fine. I'll take you home."

"Thanks."

They walked to his SUV in silence. She'd be glad to get away from the bright lights, the tempting aromas of hot dogs, burgers, funnel cake, and everything in between. But mostly she'd be glad to get away from David and the deep freeze surrounding him.

She glanced at his profile as he pulled out of the parking space. She couldn't see much in the darkened interior of the vehicle. But she could feel the distance between them. It seemed to be increasing by the second.

She glanced out the windshield. She did a double take. "You're going the wrong way," she said, as he passed the turn off for the underpass that would take them back to her apartment.

"I thought we could have a cup of coffee before I take you home."

"Fine, but next time I'd like to be asked first."

She half expected him to suggest that there wouldn't be a next time. She sighed softly in relief when he didn't.

"Fine," he said curtly. "Next time I'll ask first."

Chapter Thirteen

Diana settled into the booth across from David and wished she hadn't come. The restaurant was small, but the dim lighting and high-backed booths combined to create an intimate atmosphere that only served to emphasize the lack of intimacy between them.

He studied the menu briefly before looking up at her. "What would you like?"

"Just a cup of coffee." She closed her menu. "Decaf."

"You're sure?"

"Yes."

"I hope so, because I'm not sharing my hamburger and fries with you," he warned.

Her lips twitched several times before she laughed.

He laughed too.

She felt some of the tension leaving her body. "Okay, if you're feeling stingy, maybe I'll have a small tossed salad with low-fat French dressing."

He turned to look at the waitress. "Two hamburgers, well done with fries. No ketchup. A cup of decaf coffee, and a coke. Thanks."

"David! I said I wanted a salad," she protested after the waitress walked away.

He nodded, his eyes twinkling. "I know what you said, but I'm hungry and I'm not settling for half a burger when you decide the salad's not enough after all." He leaned forward. "You're angry with me."

She sank back in her seat, shaking her head. "Not angry."

"Then what?"

She shrugged. "Confused."

He shrugged. "So am I. I've grown used to your wanting to be with me. Now you don't. Why not?"

She shook her head. How like a man to pretend it was her fault when he was the one who'd changed. "You're far too conceited for words."

He pulled back, looking surprised. "I am? I'm not!"

She laughed. "I was only joking." She propped her chin on her hands. "Do you want to be with me?"

He nodded silently.

She wasn't satisfied. She needed him to make her believe he meant what he was saying. But if he wasn't willing to volunteer the information, she wasn't going to drag it from him word by word.

"So what do you think of the Sixers' chances of making the playoffs next year?" she asked.

They talked basketball until their burgers arrived, then they moved onto football. They were still talking about the Eagles latest draft picks as they walked back to the SUV.

She longed for him to hold her hand as he'd done on their first date, but he didn't. Inside the cab of the SUV, she turned to him. "What's wrong?"

"Nothing." He started the engine and slipped a Kenny G tape in the cassette player.

She settled in her seat. Clearly he didn't want to talk.

Ten minutes later, he pulled into the mall parking lot behind the carnival. She turned to stare at his profile. "You were supposed to be taking me home, David."

"I know, but it's time to pick up Carolyn. I'll take you home as soon as we get her." He sighed, running a hand through his hair. "Look, Diana, it doesn't have to be this way."

He sounded as if he were almost as unhappy as she was.

"The coolness between us is your doing, David."

He turned to look at her. "I need time, Diana. Just a little more time," he said quietly and slipped out of the cab.

Viewing his response as a rebuke, she didn't wait for him to help her out of the Blazer. She was out and walking away from him before he got around to her side.

He easily caught up with her, brushing the back of his hand along hers. "I know that's not what you wanted to hear."

She turned to face him. "Then why say it?"

"Because I want our relationship to be honest on every level. Is that going to be a problem?"

She shook her head silently. She was tired and just wanted to go home. Once she'd taken a long soak, she'd decide how she felt about David's new attitude toward her.

"Daddy! Diana!" Carolyn flung herself at them as they arrived at the ticket booth to find the other three waiting for them. "Did you two miss me?"

David swung her up in his arms and kissed her. "We missed you like crazy." He glanced at Diana. "Didn't we?"

"Like crazy," she echoed, kissing Carolyn's cheek.

"Why don't you kiss Daddy too since you're so close?" Carolyn demanded, giggling.

"Why not?" Diana agreed and ignoring the warning look in David's blue eyes, she pressed a lingering kiss against his cheek, close to his lips.

"On the mouth. Kiss him on the mouth, Diana," Carolyn urged.

"That's enough from you young lady," he told Carolyn as he deliberately stepped away from Diana.

Just the act of kissing his cheek served to dissipate the mounting tension between them. She laughed and turned to look at Becki and Paul, who were watching with obvious interest.

"Ah, well, if the show's over, Paul and I will be on our way," Becki said, grinning. "Thanks for letting us borrow Carolyn."

"Thank you," David said. He shifted Carolyn to his other arm and surprised Diana by catching her hand in his free one. "It's getting late. It's past Carolyn's bedtime."

"I'm not tired," Carolyn said, yawning.

Diana laughed. "Must be some other pretty little girl yawning then."

Carolyn giggled and laid her head against David's shoulder. "I am a little tired."

Carolyn was sleeping by the time David pulled up in front of her apartment. "Don't get out," she said.

"Of course I'm getting out." He took the key out of the ignition and came around to open her door.

He walked her to her door, still holding her hand. "Thanks for spending the evening with us."

She smiled up at him. "I wouldn't have been anywhere else for a million bucks."

He glanced quickly over his shoulder, toward the SUV, before bending his head to kiss her quickly on her lips. "I hope we still have a date tomorrow," he whispered against her mouth.

"You're forgetting Carolyn is coming too," she said breathlessly, resisting the urge to kiss the lips just barely touching hers.

"Not if I can get my mother to babysit, she isn't." He slipped an arm around her neck and pulled her close.

She leaned against him.

He kissed her again. As he kissed her, he caressed her back and shoulders.

She trembled in his arms and returned his kisses with equal heat.

For a moment, she enjoyed the heady sensation of knowing how deeply she could move him, then she pulled away from him. "David..."

He nibbled at her mouth. "What?"

She leaned away from him. "About tomorrow."

He leaned closer, running the tip of his tongue along her mouth. "What about it?"

"I think you'd better bring Carolyn after all."

He lifted his head and stared down at her, a question in his blue eyes. "Why? I meant it when I told you I wouldn't step over any boundaries you lay down. Don't you trust me?"

"Yes," she said quickly. "Yes, I trust you, but why take chances?"

He sighed and nodded. Raising her hand to his lips, he dropped a quick kiss in her palm. "Okay. I'll bring Carolyn. Dream of me, honey."

"Don't count on it," she warned. She heard him laughing as she closed and locked her front door.

"Sweetie, I need to talk to your Granny, so we're going to head over to her house now," David told Carolyn after finishing their Saturday morning cleaning.

"Okay, but we're not staying for dinner. We're having that with Diana. Right?" she asked anxiously.

"Right," he said.

"Did you kiss her last night, Daddy?" Carolyn asked on the drive.

He glanced at her in the rearview mirror. Something in her voice told him she already knew the answer. "Yes," he said briefly.

She giggled. "And did you like it?"

Carolyn had either awaken while he was with Diana at the door or had never been asleep in the first place. "I've told you all I'm going to tell you about it, Sweetcakes," he said firmly.

"I'll bet you did," she said smugly. "I couldn't see too good. How many times did you kiss her? And did she kiss you back?"

"Carolyn," he said in a warning voice.

"Oh, all right," she said, not sounding in the least subdued. "I was only asking."

"It's none of your business."

"But it is. Don't I have any say in who you kiss?"

His lips twitched. "No, you don't."

"But what if you decide to just kiss any woman and like it and want to marry her?"

He smiled. "I don't just kiss anyone and you know it."

"Then that makes Diana special!" she said triumphantly. "So are you going to marry her, Daddy?"

His smile vanished. "I don't want you to count on that. I like her a lot, sweetie, but..."

"But what, Daddy? You said you were going to get married again, so why not to Diana?"

Why not to Diana, indeed? She and Carolyn got along well. He enjoyed being with her. And he couldn't imagine meeting anyone else who occupied his thoughts nearly as much as she did. She would be good for both him and Carolyn. So why not give Carolyn what they both wanted? Which was Diana in his life, in his arms, and in his bed.

He glanced at Carolyn in the rearview mirror. This time he made brief eye contact with her and smiled warmly at her.

"Oh, Daddy! Thank you! Thank you!"

"Don't get ahead of yourself, Carolyn. I haven't said I'll ask her to marry me yet. And even if I do, she might say no."

"Get real, Daddy!" Carolyn said happily. "She'll say yes. She loves us and we love her. Right, Daddy?"

"We're fond of her," he said carefully. "And this little conversation is just between you and me. Okay?"

"You mean I can't even tell Diana?"

"That's exactly what I mean. I don't want you telling anyone. Remember, I haven't said I'm going to ask her."

"You will," she said.

At his mother's house, Carolyn ran into the den to play the video game his mother had bought her as a just-because-I-love-you gift, while he sat in the living room with his mother. He took a few sips of the tea she'd poured, then got up and paced in front of the big glass-topped coffee table.

"What's wrong, dear?" she asked when he came to a stop in front of the large bay window.

"Nothing. Everything's fine." He took a deep breath, then blew it out. "Mom, how long was it before you knew you wanted to marry Dad?"

"Oh. Well, dear, I knew the moment we met. He didn't know I was the one, but I knew he was. Just as I think Diana's known from the moment you two met that you were the one for her. It's taken you a little longer, hasn't it?"

He continued to stare out the window. "I loved Harriet."

He heard her moving before he felt her hand on his arm, her cheek pressed briefly against the back of his shoulder. "And she loved you, but life goes on, dear."

"I know, but it hasn't been that long since—"

"There's no set time for mourning, David. Harriet loved you too. She'd want you to be happy. She wouldn't want you to let a woman who loves you slip away just because you thought you hadn't waited long enough. She'd want you to be happy with Diana."

"I've only known her a few weeks. It took several months for me to be sure enough of Harriet to know I wanted to marry her."

"You were younger then," she pointed out. "You didn't know what love was."

He turned to face her. "Don't misunderstand, Mom. I haven't said I love her. I like her a lot."

She stared up into his eyes. "You're telling me you'd marry a woman you don't love?"

"I haven't said I am marrying her."

"Oh, David, let's not play games." She placed her palms against his chest. "Are you going to ask her to marry you?"

"I don't know."

"David!"

"I don't know," he insisted. "And your giving me that disapproving look isn't going to change that."

"What is?" she asked gently.

He shook his head. "Things are moving too rapidly. I need a little time and a little space."

"And what if Diana meets someone else while you're getting your time and space?"

The thought left a sick feeling in his stomach. "You've just finished telling me that she loves me," he countered. "She'll wait."

"Oh, David, don't be too sure of her. She's a warm, beautiful woman."

"That any man would be glad to know. I know," he said wearily. "I'm very glad to know her, but I just need time."

Diana spent Saturday cooking. For Carolyn, who was a picky eater, she made a small tossed salad, Cream of Spinach soup, a peanut butter and strawberry cream cheese sandwich, and Butter Almond cookies for dessert. For herself and David, she made a Cucumber salad, Asparagus soup, chicken chops with sausage stuffing, and a baked medley of string beans, corn, and new potatoes. For dessert, she made a pineapple upside-down cake.

By the time she finished cooking, it was four o'clock and she felt like one big knot of tension. She spent an hour in a warm bath, relaxing before she dressed.

She chose a modest, short-sleeved, two-piece silk dress which swirled becomingly around her calves when she moved. She sprayed herself with her favorite scent and slipped on a pair of heels. Studying her reflection she decided she would do quite nicely. Hopefully, David would think so as well.

He and Carolyn arrived a little before six.

"Wow! You look real pretty!" Carolyn said, gaping at her. "Doesn't she, Daddy?"

"Oh, yes, she does," David said softly. He held a bouquet of pink carnations. "For you, pretty lady."

Carolyn giggled and Diana's cheeks burned as she accepted the carnations. "Thank you. Come in and have a seat while I put these in water." She glanced over her shoulder. "Can I get either of you anything to drink?"

"Do you have any strawberry milk?" Carolyn asked.

Diana groaned silently. How could she have forgotten how much the child loved strawberry milk? "No, but I did make you some strawberry Kool-Aid. Will that do?"

"Okay. I'll come with you," Carolyn said, slipping off the sofa where she'd been sitting with her father.

Diana smiled at David and felt her heart beat quicken when he smiled back, his gaze warm and lingering. "I ... I'll be right back," she said slowly.

"I'll be waiting," he told her.

She turned away, suddenly certain that everything was going to be all right between them.

They had a noisy, laughter-filled meal. Carolyn's happy mood was infectious. Before long, all three of them were laughing at the most insignificant things. Diana watched with satisfaction as David and Carolyn devoured the food she'd prepared with such care.

After dinner, they sat Carolyn on a stool close to the sink and the three of them washed the dishes.

"Oh, this is so nice," Carolyn said suddenly. "I wish we could always be together like this. Just the three of us."

Diana felt David's gaze on her. She looked up to find him watching her. The look in his eyes made her catch her breath. It was warm and...dare she hope, loving? If he'd only reconcile with God, she'd feel that her prayers had finally been answered.

"Maybe we can be," he said.

She blinked and stared at him over Carolyn's head. For him to make the suggestion in Carolyn's hearing indicated how serious he was. "What...what did...you say...?"

"He said maybe we can be," Carolyn piped in. "Maybe my daddy likes you a whole lot. Maybe he wants to—"

"Maybe he wants to speak for himself, young lady," David interrupted, dragging his gaze away from Diana to look down at Carolyn.

"Then speak, David," she urged softly.

"Yeah, Daddy. Speak."

He lifted Carolyn off the stool and set her gently on her feet. "I want to talk to Diana alone, sweetie. Will you wait in the living room?"

"No, Daddy! I want to stay and hear what you have to say and what she has to say. And if you're going to kiss her, I want to watch."

"Wait in the living room, Sweetie," he repeated, turning his warm gaze back to Diana's heated cheeks.

"Oh, all right, but—"

"No buts. Just go, Carolyn."

Carolyn made a face, but slowly left the kitchen.

"You wanted to talk," Diana prodded when he stared silently at her long after Carolyn had left the room.

"When we're alone."

"We are alone."

He shook his head. "No. I mean without Carolyn listening at the door."

"I'm not listening at the door! I'm in the hallway!"

Diana was startled into laughter at the sound of Carolyn's indignant voice coming from the hallway. "I see what you mean."

"Have dinner with me tomorrow?"

"Tomorrow? I should...that's the night I usually visit the shut-ins."

"I'll come with you. We can talk between visits."

"I don't usually go alone."

He grinned at her. "You won't be alone. I'll be with you."

She laughed. "Actually, that's not what I meant. But I'm sure I can rearrange things just this once."

"Then what's the problem?"

"No problem. It's just that on these visits, we usually talk about the Lord and read a few scriptures."

He shrugged. "You say that as if you think I don't want to hear about Him."

"Do you, David? Are you beginning to feel better about what happened to your wife?"

He compressed his lips. "No. Nothing can make me feel better about that, but I am feeling better about life in general. I'm feeling more inclined to talk to and hear about God since I met you."

"Oh, David!" She reached out and squeezed his hand. "Maybe you won't wait for the gospel concert to come to church with me."

He lifted her hand to his lips and pressed several warm kisses in her palm before looking up into her eyes. "Maybe I won't."

Chapter Fourteen

David arrived with a dozen roses for their date the following night.

"Oh, David! They're beautiful!" Diana said.

He brushed the back of his hand against her cheek. "So are you."

The warm look in his blue gaze made her feel weak-kneed. She clutched the roses against her breasts. "They're beautiful," she said again. "And they're red."

He laughed and dropped a casual kiss against her cheek. "I know what color they are. I'm the guy who brought them, remember?"

She paused. "A man doesn't just give a woman red roses on the spur of the moment."

"Doesn't he?"

"No. Do you know what red roses mean?"

He nodded silently, still smiling down at her.

Afraid to read too much into the roses or his response to her question, she flashed him a quick smile. "Then I don't need to tell you."

"No, Diana, you don't."

"Let me put these in water and then we have to go. I told Mrs. Wilson we'd be there around seven."

"Okay," he said, linking his fingers with hers. "Let's go."

She disengaged her hand, put the roses in a vase, set the vase on the hall table before leaving her apartment with him.

The moment the door was locked, he reclaimed her hand. He bent to kiss the corner of her mouth before he helped her into his SUV.

She tingled all over and had to resist the urge to turn to him with her lips parted and her face lifted in a shameless appeal for a real kiss.

She was very conscious of him sitting next to her on the fifteen minute drive to Mary Wilson's house. She glanced at his hands resting on the wheel and imagined them cupping her face or holding her close as he kissed her. Her desire for such intimacy with him shamed her.

She moistened her lips and turned her gaze forward. "Turn left at the corner," she said. "Then it's the third house on the right."

He pulled into the driveway of a small, single home and turned to look at her. "Here we are."

She nodded.

"Is there anything I should know about her?"

"Mrs. Wilson is older and used to speaking her mind. Don't be offended by anything she might say," she warned.

"Don't worry, Diana. I have a grandmother who delights in shocking people by speaking her mind."

She suppressed a frown. How could he be so cool and calm when she was so nervous? Unless his heart wasn't nearly as engaged with her as hers was with him. Or worse, had he decided he didn't want to follow through on his hints of the night before? Shouldn't a man on the verge of proposing be nervous? "I didn't know you had a grandmother, David."

He smiled. "There's a lot you don't know about me."

"Yes," she agreed coolly. "Mainly because you won't tell me anything."

"I'll tell you anything you want to know," he said calmly. "Anything at all. So knock yourself out asking."

"Yeah, well, maybe I'm not so interested in knowing anymore," she said, feeling the need to be disagreeable.

He arched a brow, smiling. "I hope that's not true."

It was clear he wasn't going to allow her to pick a fight with him. She wasn't even sure why she was trying to. "Never mind. Mrs. Wilson will be waiting so we'd better go in."

Just for a moment, when he helped her out of the SUV, he stood very close to her, holding her hand while he stared down at her.

She stared breathlessly back, until he parted his lips and bent his head. He was going to kiss her. If he did, he'd scatter what little wits she had left. Besides Mary Wilson was almost certainly watching from her window.

"Don't," she said and tugged on her hand.

"Why not?"

"Mrs. Wilson is old-fashioned. I wouldn't want her to think I stand around making out in public."

With a sigh of what she imagined was frustration, he released her hand. "Fine." He silently followed her inside.

Mary Wilson took one look at David and patted the seat on a big, over-stuffed teal sofa beside her. "Well isn't this nice? You must be Diana's young man."

Diana shot David a quick look, shaking her head. "Oh, no. He's not."

"Oh, yes," he said, taking the proffered seat beside the older woman. "I am."

"I knew there must be a man in the picture when she started sparkling," Mary Wilson went on. "And such a handsome one too. You're a perfect foil for Diana."

David arched a brow and smiled at Diana.

She compressed her lips.

"You two will make beautiful kids together."

David laughed.

Diana's cheeks burned as she thought of having his baby. It was all downhill after that. At least for Diana. She sat with a forced smile on her face as David and Mary Wilson discussed her as if she weren't there.

Mary Wilson gave a satisfied nod of her gray head. "As soon as I saw you two standing by your truck outside, I knew you must be the reason she's been looking more beautiful than usual."

David glanced at her again. "She is beautiful."

"She is, and I hope you realize what a good deal you're getting with her," she told David. "Diana's a beautiful young woman ripe for marriage."

She felt the hot blood heat her cheeks.

David smiled. "Is she?"

"Oh, yes. And she has everything a man could want in a wife," Mary Wilson went on. "In addition to being pretty, she's sweet-tempered, has a good sense of humor, and she can cook. That's important. Many of these so-modern women doesn't seem to understand a man wants a hot meal when he gets home at night."

"You're absolutely right, ma'am," David said, ignoring the annoyed look Diana shot his way. "I'm obviously fortunate that she even noticed me."

"Yes, you are, but I can see why she did," Mary Wilson said, squinting at him through her glasses. "You're a good looking young man."

"Thank you," he said, his eyes gleaming with amusement.

"Now how long have you two been see—"

"Ah, we didn't come here to talk about ourselves," Diana interrupted. "We came to see what you needed. What we could do for you?"

"Nothing, dear. I'm fine. Reverend Howard and his wife stopped by yesterday and bought some groceries and sat with me. Oh, we had a lovely visit."

"There must be something we can do for you," Diana said.

"You are very sweet, Diana." She turned to David. "You know you're getting a very sweet girl in Diana."

David nodded, his gaze briefly locking with Diana's. "Yes, I know," he said quietly. His gaze rested briefly on her lips. "Very sweet."

Diana's heartbeat a little faster.

"Good." Mary Wilson patted David's hand. "I can see you two are anxious to be alone, so I'll let you go."

"Oh, we're in no rush to be alone," Diana said, panicking at the thought of being alone with David.

Mary Wilson smiled and got to her feet. "She's shy. A pleasant thing in a girl, don't you think, David?"

"Oh, absolutely," David agreed meekly, getting to his feet. "And you're right. We would like to be alone."

Mary Wilson glanced at Diana's bare left hand. "Come see me again when you two make it official, David."

"I'll do that."

"Then run along and have fun together."

Five minutes later, Diana sat staring out the windshield of the SUV.

David got in beside her. "Where to now?" he asked, starting the engine.

She turned to stare at his profile. "You shouldn't have told her you were my...that you were mine," she said in a tight voice.

He turned to look at her. "Why not?"

"Because it isn't true, David."

For a moment he was silent before he cut the engine. "It could be if you wanted it that way," he suggested softly.

"What I want, David, is to be taken home."

"Okay," he said, sounding disappointed. "But have coffee with me first. I want to talk to you."

The way things were going for her, he probably wanted to tell her he needed space. And if he did, she'd be hard pressed not to slap him so hard he would see the proverbial stars. "What about?"

"Come and find out," he said. "Yes? No?"

"I am not in the mood to be teased, David!" she snapped.

"So who's teasing?"

"David!"

"Hey! Come on, honey." He leaned forward to brush his lips against her cheek, close to the corner of her mouth. "I have no intentions of teasing you."

She leaned away from him. "Then stop trying to kiss me and tell me what you want to talk about. Now. Right here."

"I'd rather not."

She pushed at his shoulder and he moved back into his seat. "And I'd rather you did."

"Fine," he said, sounding annoyed. "I wanted to set the stage to make this romantic, but have it your way, Diana."

Her heart beat quickened. Was he about to propose? "Make what romantic?"

"I was wondering..." He cupped her cheek in one big hand, pressing the ball of his thumb against her bottom lip. "Hoping...will you marry me, Diana?"

"Will I...what?"

"I want to marry you. Do you want to marry me?"

Her eyes filled with tears. She sucked in a deep gasping breath before she turned to throw her arms around his neck. All the reasons why she should refuse flew out of her head and she nodded wildly. "Yes! Yes! Oh, David, yes, I will marry you!"

He returned her embrace and she felt his warm lips brushing her forehead, her cheek, and finally her neck.

She trembled.

They clung to each other for several moments before he cupped her face between his palms. "Yes?"

"Yes, David. Yes."

He slipped an arm around her waist and lifted her face.

She closed her eyes and parted her lips with the tip of her tongue extended.

With one arm around her waist and the other palm cupping the back of her neck, he pressed several long, heated kisses against her mouth. He kissed her until she was breathless. When she tore her mouth away from his, he burned his lips against the side of her neck.

She gasped, feeling hot and greedy for a pleasure they had no right to share until after they were married. But her prayers had finally been answered. She was going to be his wife. Tears slid down her cheeks.

"Hey." He lifted his head to look down at her. "I was hoping you'd be happy. Why are you crying?"

"I am happy."

He pressed a sweet kiss against her mouth. "Then stop crying." He wiped her tears away with the tips of his thumbs. "Please. I hate to see you in tears. Even happy ones."

"Oh, David!" She stroked her fingers through his hair. "I love you! I knew I would the moment I saw you."

He smiled and kissed her nose. "Then you won't keep me waiting long? I would really like to marry you very soon."

"Soon? How soon? Why soon?" she asked, visions of a big, formal wedding filling her head.

"This is why," he whispered. He drew her into his arms and kissed her.

She closed her eyes, melting into him. She returned his kisses with a heat that matched his. Within moments, she burned with desire and need.

He trailed a series of light kisses down the side of her neck.

She trembled. "David..."

He stroked his fingers down from her neck, igniting her passions. She couldn't muster the resolve or will to stop him—even when he cupped his hands over her breasts. She gasped, feeling a coil of heat in her belly.

It was David who finally pulled away from her. "I...I'm sorry," he said, his voice raspy, his breathing uneven. "I lost my head. Forgive me. It won't happen again."

She stared silently at him, her cheeks feverish with embarrassment and shame at her failure to stop him. How far would she have allowed him to go before she protested?

He slipped back into his seat. His hands shook on the steering wheel.

She glanced out the window at the quiet street. She saw Mary Wilson's curtain lowered. Oh, Lord, what would she think of Diana now? "We should go, David. We're a little old to get a citation for necking in public."

He laughed and turned to look at her. "You're probably right. When will you marry me?"

"I can't think about anything now except how happy I am!" She reached out to caress his right hand. "I just want to savor this moment. Besides, I thought you needed time."

"What I need is you as my wife ASAP." He lifted her hand to his mouth and kissed her palm. "Part of me knew I was yours the first time we met."

"You didn't know any such thing."

"I did — deep down."

"So deep you didn't know it?" She suggested.

He laughed. "Never mind that. When will you marry me?"

"I need time to lose a little weight first. At least—"

"No!" His hand tightened on hers until it hurt. "Not an ounce."

She stared at him. "David?"

"I want every beautiful, delightful, sassy, breathtaking pound, inch, and ounce of you. There's not a single thing about you that I would change even if I could."

She knew he meant it. "Oh, you're a darling!" Her eyes filled with fresh tears. "My darling."

He grinned at her. "I can't think of anything I want more than to be your darling, Diana."

"Oh, David, you are!" she whispered and kissed him with an intensity he returned so eagerly that they were soon wrapped in each other's arms devouring each other's lips.

As before, it was David who finally pulled away. "Sweetheart, please! Control yourself," he said with tender humor. "Remember, I have my reputation to consider."

"Sorry, love, but you go to my head," she told him truthfully.

He started the SUV and drove away. "I know the feeling, sweetheart."

Chapter Fifteen

Her doubts began that night as she lay in bed recalling every moment of their evening. Why had he proposed? Just three days earlier, he'd told her he needed time. He still wore his wedding ring. And he hadn't offered her an engagement ring. Who proposed without a ring?

She realized with a sudden chill that he hadn't once said he loved her. The warmth of his kisses and the ardor of his embrace told her that he wanted her physically. But there had been nothing in his manner to indicate that his desire was motivated by love. Most importantly, he hadn't yet fully reconciled with the Lord. How could she possibly marry him before he had?

She decided the only thing to do was to come right out and ask him why he wanted to marry her. She also needed to know what he intended to do to repair his relationship with God. She got out of bed and called to invite him to dinner on Tuesday night.

She was surprised when he arrived for dinner with Carolyn. "Carolyn, what a nice surprise." She lifted her gaze to look at him.

He shrugged. "She wanted to come."

Carolyn frowned. "Didn't you want me, Diana?"

"Of course I wanted you," she replied promptly.

Carolyn threw her arms around her legs and proceeded to gush over how happy she was that her Daddy was finally going to marry her Diana.

There was no opportunity to talk with Carolyn there.

"We'll have dinner Thursday and talk then," he promised as they stood at her door saying good night, while Carolyn sat waiting in the SUV.

Diana nodded. "Okay."

He bent and kissed the corner of her mouth. "Dream of me."

"Don't count on it," she told him, smiling.

He caressed her cheek and left.

Thursday night after dinner at the Riverfront restaurant, they walked hand in hand along the pier. She was silent, trying to decide the best approach to take when she asked him why he wanted to marry her.

He stopped suddenly and touched her face. "Where are you? Come back to me."

She leaned into him, tilting her face up so she could look into his eyes. "David, are you sure you want to marry me?"

He slipped his arms around her waist. "I've never been surer of anything in my life."

"Never?" Surely he'd wanted to marry Harriet more.

"Never," he repeated. "When are you going to marry me?"

"You're rushing me," she protested, pressing her hands against his chest to discourage him from drawing her even closer into his embrace. "It takes time to arrange a wedding. There are so many things to do and I don't even have a ring yet," she reminded him.

"A wedding?"

"Yes. That's what people have when they get married," she teased.

"You mean as in a formal one with ushers and bridesmaids, and an endless wait until you're my wife?" His arms slackened. "Oh, Diana! Not that again."

She shoved against his chest.

He released her.

"That's exactly what I mean. I know you've been there and done that, but this will be the first time for me," she reminded him in a small, hurt voice. "If you think I'm going to be satisfied with anything less, you're wrong!"

He sighed and ran both hands through his hair. "I was hoping you'd want to marry me sooner than all that. That's all I meant, sweetheart. If you want a big formal wedding, then we'll have a big, formal wedding."

"Why?" She stared at him with tears in her eyes, willing him to say because he loved her.

He shrugged. "It's your day. I just want to marry you."

She leaned on the railing over the river and stared into the dark water below, afraid to ask the questions she so badly wanted answered.

His hands came down on the railing near hers and she felt his hard warmth against her back, imprisoning her between the railing and his body.

She shivered as she felt his lips brushing against the side of her neck. "What's wrong, sweetheart?"

She turned in his embrace and looked up at him. "I love you."

He pressed a gentle, tender kiss against her mouth.

She closed her eyes on a flood of tears. He didn't love her. Worst, he still hadn't made peace with the Lord.

"Do you have any plans for this Saturday?" he asked, lifting his head.

She shook her head.

"Good. Then we can go looking for your ring Saturday."

A man who loved the woman he wanted to marry would have done that himself. "I thought you'd pick it out yourself."

"I thought it might be nice if we did it together, but if you'd rather I did it alone, I—"

"No. Picking one out together is a great idea." She ran a finger over his left hand and felt the ring on his third finger. What would be nicer still was picking out one for him.

He caressed her cheek. "Is there something else bothering you?"

Now was the time to tell him she couldn't set a date until he'd reconciled with God, but she found that her courage had deserted her. She shook her head. "No."

He stared down into her eyes for several long moments. Then he kissed her cheek. "I'll do my best to be a good husband and make you happy, Diana."

She slipped her arms around his waist and buried her face against his shoulder. "And I'll try very hard to make you happy."

"You only need to marry me, and I'll be happy," he told her, returning her embrace.

That would probably be true if he loved her.

He sighed. "Now let's talk about this formal wedding you and I are going to have."

She looked up at him. "Are you sure you want that?"

"I want you, Diana. Nothing more. Nothing less."

He was probably stretching the truth, but as far as she was concerned, his answer was completely satisfying.

"Why can't I go, too?"

It was Saturday morning. David and Carolyn were in the Blazer, heading for his mother's house, where he would be leaving her while he and Diana went to pick out her ring.

"Because this is something that Diana and I need to do alone."

"Are there going to be a lot of things you two are going to want to do without me, Daddy?"

He winced at the anxiety in Carolyn's voice. He turned on his left turn signal, guided the SUV out of traffic, turned onto a quiet street, and turned off the engine.

He unbuckled his seat belt, got out of the front seat and slipped into the back next to Carolyn. "Sweetie, you are the most important person to me in the whole world."

"Even more important than Diana?"

"Yes. Even more important than her, sweetie. I love you more than anyone else in the world. When Diana and I are married, some things will change for you and me, but not that."

"What kind of things, Daddy?" she asked, her voice and eyes full of anxiety.

"Well, for one thing, you're going to have to knock and wait to be told it's okay before you come into my—our bedroom."

"But Daddy, I always come into your room without knocking."

"I know, sweetie." He stroked her hair. "but that'll have to change."

"I don't want it to change. Maybe I don't want you to marry her after all!"

He cupped her face in his hands and kissed her on the tip of her nose. "You don't mean that, sweetie."

"I do because I don't want things to change between me and you, Daddy! I want you to stay my Daddy!"

"None of the things that really matter will change. I'll always be your daddy and love you more than anyone else in the world. My being married to Diana will make us both happier. There will be adjustments at first, but they'll be worth it because we both want her to be a part of our lives. Yes?"

"Yes...I guess, Daddy."

"And I promise you that Diana and I will try to include you in almost everything we do from now on."

"Why not everything, Daddy?"

"Because just like you and I like to be alone, sometimes a husband and wife like to be alone too."

"Daddy, will you still want to be alone with me when you're married to Diana?"

He released her seat belt, wrapped his arms around her and, lifted her out of her seat, holding her close to his heart. "Yes, sweetie, I will. Most of the time the three of us will be together. But sometimes, it'll be just you and me. Okay?"

"Okay, Daddy."

He settled her back in her seat and fastened her seat belt. "All right now, sweetie?"

She nodded. "Yes, Daddy. I guess you can marry Diana after all."

"Thank you, sweetie."

Diana was dismayed when David told her of Carolyn's fear on the drive to jeweler's row in downtown Philadelphia an hour later. "So we'll have to shower her with extra attention for a while until she realizes how much we both love her."

He pulled into an underground parking lot and turned to look at her. "That's not going to be a problem, is it?"

"Of course not." Although she spoke quickly, a sense of disquiet filled her. Was Carolyn's sudden change of heart a sign from the Lord that Diana was acting out of harmony with His will for her? What right had she to agree to marry a man whose faith had wavered? The scriptures clearly said Christians should marry only in the Lord. Was David, in his present state of spiritual distress, "in the Lord?"

He leaned over and kissed her cheek. "Thanks."

She looked at his hands resting on the steering wheel. Her gaze locked on the gold band on his ring finger. "I brought my credit card," she said slowly.

He arched a brow. "Why? We're not going Dutch on your ring, Diana."

"I know." She reached across his body to lay her hand over his left one. "I thought we could exchange rings when we're married, David."

His eyes widened, his lips parted, and he stared at her in silence.

She stared back.

He pulled his hand from underneath hers. "This bothers you?" he asked in a flat voice, touching his wedding band.

"No," she lied. "I just want to give you a ring."

"Fine." He hesitated a moment, sighed softly, then slipped the ring off his finger. He put it in his jacket pocket. Was it her imagination or did the smile he turn on her hold very little warmth? "I'd be delighted to wear your ring."

"Why don't I believe you mean that, David?"

His eyes narrowed. "Probably because you don't love or trust me nearly as much as you claim to," he retorted. "I told you once before that I usually say exactly what I mean. That hasn't changed. If I tell you I'd be delighted to wear your ring, that's exactly what I mean."

Her eyes filled with tears. "Then why were you so reluctant to take that one off?"

He looked at the tears glistening in her eyes and sighed. "I've worn it a long time," he said, his voice softening. "It was a gift of love from Harriet which symbolized our...it meant a lot to me. I cherished it even more after her death." He stroked her cheek tenderly. "Just as I will cherish the one you give me."

"Oh, David! I'm sorry!" she whispered.

He gave her a brief hug. "Don't be sorry. Just love me and be patient with me."

She didn't really have a choice. "I do love you."

He kissed her cheek. "Let's go get our rings."

They spent three hours at four different jewelry shops before they settled on a diamond solitaire in a diamond-cut gold setting. Diana paid for the matching wedding band for David.

Looking up into his eyes as she tried it on his finger, she could see nothing but warmth and promise in his smiling gaze. She sighed happily. Maybe it was the Lord's will for them to be man and wife. She hugged the thought to her.

When they left the jeweler's, she felt as if she were floating. She couldn't stop staring down at the ring sparkling on her finger. She was so happy. Surely the Lord didn't mean to deprive her of this great joy.

"You'd better watch where you're going," David warned, amusement in his voice as he steered her around a pole she was about to walk into.

She stopped in the middle of the sidewalk and slipped her arms around his waist. "Oh, David! I'm so happy."

"So I am, sweetheart, but we'd better be happy somewhere else," he said, pressing closer to her to allow another couple to squeeze pass them. He took her hand in his. "Let's go eat. Then I want to be alone with you."

"Where?"

"Home. I want to show it to you."

She wasn't sure how she felt about seeing the house he'd shared so happily with Harriet, but she was about to find out.

"Home" for David and Carolyn was a big, two-storied single house with a large open porch and a second floor balcony, which she imagined led off the master bedroom.

"What do you think? Could you live here with Carolyn and me?"

He sounded anxious and she realized he was probably afraid she'd insist they start their married life living in a different house. That was her inclination.

She leaned back against him, her gaze still on the house. "It's very nice from out here. Let's go inside."

After an inspection of the house, Diana stood in the middle of the living room, feeling as if the wind had been knocked out of her. It was a large room with pale blue walls, dark blue woodwork, a beautiful pale blue ceiling fan, deep, comfortable contemporary sofas and chairs, and no less than four pictures of Harriet Jordan. Over the mantelpiece was a large family portrait of David, Harriet, and Carolyn.

He couldn't be serious. There was no way she could live in the same house he and Harriet had shared. There would be too many memories for her to compete with. Not to mention too many pictures of her.

There were three other pictures of Harriet Jordan downstairs. One on each end table, and one on the wall at the base of the wide, curving staircase.

Diana bit her lip. She felt oppressed by all the pictures of the smiling, beautiful, slender Harriet Jordan. How could she possibly compete with her memories?

"We can redo the whole house from top to bottom," he told her, as they stood together in the master bedroom. The walls here were a light rose, the woodwork mauve. "New wallpaper, furniture. We'll buy new furniture and redecorate everything, except Carolyn's bedroom."

She moved across the room to look out onto the balcony. She could see a big, overstuffed chaise lounge through the French doors. How many times had David lay there with Harriet in his arms telling her he loved her?

She felt a spark of jealousy and turned away, only to find herself facing the bed. Her gaze shifted to the nightstand. There was yet another picture of Harriet Jordan's smiling face staring back at her. She quickly turned to face the balcony again. How could he expect her to live with him in this house that reeked of the love he and Harriet had shared?

"Diana?"

She felt his arms slipping around her, drawing her back against him. He nuzzled her neck, making her tingle. "I know it's asking a lot, but you can change it anyway you like. We can even enlarge one of the other rooms and make it into the master bedroom."

That wasn't going to be enough. She couldn't live with him there.

"It's the only home Carolyn's ever known," he said, when she remained silent. "She says she feels as if her mommy's not totally gone when she's here."

She turned in his arms to face him. "Then how can I change anything? David, it's not fair to expect me to live here with you without changes."

"I know. I know." He stroked her cheek. "I'll talk to Carolyn and make her understand. We'll keep her room just as it is, but the rest ... we'll redo any way you want, Diana. Any way at all."

She had a sinking feeling Carolyn wasn't the only one who didn't feel as if Harriet wasn't totally gone when he was in this house. Why else would he have so many pictures of her?

Agreeing to live in this house would be a bad idea, but the humble, pleading look in his eyes undid her. How could she say no when she loved him so much? Wasn't part of loving someone doing the things which pleased them, even if you weren't necessarily pleased yourself?

She leaned up and kissed his chin. "Oh, David, don't look like that. I...I'll live here with you and Carolyn, but there will definitely have to be major changes."

"Fine. Whatever you want. Thank you!" His arms tightened around her.

Even as she lifted her lips to accept the grateful kisses he pressed against her mouth, she wondered if she were digging a deep hole for herself by agreeing to live there with him.

Chapter Sixteen

The next three weeks were bittersweet for Diana. She either saw or talked to David nearly every day. She went down on her knees in heartfelt thanks to God when he and Carolyn accompanied her to Sunday service on three consecutive Sundays. And when he remained in the church speaking to the pastor after the service, she knew at least part of her prayer was in the process of being answered. When they were together, she felt confident that everything would be all right. But the moment he left her side, she'd remember his house, filled with pictures of Harriet, and her doubts returned.

It was Harriet's face he saw just before he went to sleep. She probably haunted his dreams. Diana began to fear he might even think of Harriet when he kissed her. How could she marry a man who didn't love her? If only he'd tell her he loved her! Even if it wasn't true, she longed to hear the words.

She worried and prayed over her indecision until she felt sick. When David asked to see her one Monday night, three weeks after their official engagement, she told him she had other plans and called his mother.

"Diana, dear, this is a nice surprise. How are you?"

"I. need to talk to you."

"Oh, dear, you sound upset. How can I help?"

"May I come to your home?"

"Yes, dear, of course."

"I'll see you in twenty minutes."

Gloria Jordan met her at the door, took one look at her, and drew Diana into her arms. All the misery and uncertainties welled up in her for the past three weeks burst forth and she sobbed on the older woman's shoulder.

"Oh, my dear! My dear!"

Diana felt soft, comforting hands stroking her hair and face and struggled to get control of herself. She lifted her head and looked at her. "I'm sorry."

"No, dear. Don't be sorry for coming to me." She gently wiped Diana's face, took her hand, and led her into the living room. She sat in a high backed Queen Anne chair and Diana sat next to her.

"What is it, dear?" Gloria asked, stroking her hair.

"I can't marry him!"

"Oh, my dear!" Gloria's hand stilled on her hair. "What's happened?"

"He doesn't love me."

"Of course he does."

Gloria spoke with such confidence, that Diana lifted her head and stared up at her. "Did he tell you he did?"

"No," she admitted with obvious reluctance. "But he's my son. I know him. He wouldn't marry a woman he didn't love."

"He still loves Harriet."

"Harriet is dead, dear."

"Why don't you tell him that?" she cried wildly, jumping to her feet. "Three weeks ago, he was still wearing the ring she gave him. He has pictures of her all over the house he expects me to live in. And worse of all, he hasn't once … not once said he loves me!"

"Sometimes men have a hard time expressing their love—"

"I'm sure he didn't have any problem telling Harriet he loved her. Why should I settle for less? And then there's the question of his spirituality. No matter how much I love him, I can't marry a man who doesn't love God."

"He does love God! He's been to service with you for the last three weeks and he's started to read the Bible again to Carolyn at night. He told me yesterday that he's made arrangements to have private meetings once a week with our pastor."

"I'm very glad that his relationship with the Lord is on the mend, but that doesn't change things between us." She took several deep breaths, stared down at the ring on her finger, and then tugged it off. Fresh tears filled her eyes and she walked over to lay it in Gloria's palm. "I know it's the cowardly way, but I can't face him. Please, give this to him for me."

"Oh, no, Diana! Please. Just talk to him. Tell him how you feel."

"I've tried, but I can't. Whenever I try talking to him, he starts kissing me and by the time he stops, I'm ready to agree to anything he says. Please. I know it's not right, and it's not fair to you, but I can't face him. Please give this to him for me."

"All right, I'll tell him."

"Thank you. I...I'm sorry for all the trouble I caused."

Gloria shook her head. "You haven't caused any trouble, dear. I can understand how you feel. I just wish you'd talk to him before you make up your mind."

"It's already made up. If he loved me, he had plenty of chances to say so, but he never has."

"Why else would he marry you?"

Thoughts of the passion in his lips and hands as they caressed and kissed her, made Diana blush with shame. "He wants me and he knows that marriage is the only way he can have me. But that has nothing to do with love. I need him to love me. I'm sorry. I have to go," she whispered and hurried out of the house.

David stared down at the ring his mother had placed in his palm with a feeling of numbness. The moment she'd called, after eight, to tell him she was driving over to talk to him, he'd known she had bad news. But not this bad.

"Why do you want to marry Diana, David?"

Anger slowly replaced the numbness. "What difference does it make? She's clearly already decided why she thinks I did."

"It makes a difference to me, David. I told her that you loved her. I told her you wouldn't have asked her to marry you if you didn't."

He turned away and went to stare out the window onto the lawn. "And she didn't believe you."

"She wanted to hear it from you. That's not asking too much, David. I heard you tell Harriet you loved her on countless occasions."

"So?"

"So why couldn't you tell Diana the same thing?"

He swung around to face his mother. "Why couldn't she trust me? I took off my wedding band for her. I removed Harriet's pictures everywhere except Carolyn's room. I told her she could change the house anyway she liked! Why wasn't that enough for her? What does she want from me?"

"She wants to know that you love her, David! She needs to hear you say it. I know you love her. Why won't you tell her?"

"Why should I tell her anything?" he demanded angrily.

"Because you'll lose her if you don't."

He clenched his hand on Diana's ring until he felt the diamond biting into his palm. "Maybe that wouldn't be such a loss after all. I don't need a wife who doesn't trust me."

She shook her head. "You don't mean that, David. I know you don't."

He backed away when she moved to touch him. "Mom, if you don't mind, I want to be alone."

"I do mind. You're upset. You need—"

"What I need is to be alone to think."

"And pray, David. Don't you think it's past time you had a heart to heart with God?"

"Please, Mom. Let me walk you to your car."

She hesitated before she finally nodded. Outside, he opened her car door and she slipped in. Her driver side window slid down. "You know where I am if you need me or want to talk."

"I know. Thanks for everything, Mom." He leaned in and kissed her cheek.

He waited until her car disappeared down the street before going back in the house.

He was surprised to find Carolyn standing on the stairs, clutching her stuffed Big Bird, staring down at him. "Daddy, I thought I heard Granny. Is something wrong?"

Carolyn would be devastated when she learned he and Diana weren't going to be married after all.

Slipping the ring in his pants pocket, he scooped her up in his arms and carried her back upstairs. "Nothing's wrong, sweetie. Now back to bed with you."

She stared up into his face as he tucked her in. "Daddy, are you sure nothing's wrong? You look ... funny."

He wouldn't tell her about Diana until he absolutely had to. He kissed her cheek and stood up. "I'm fine, sweetie. Go back to sleep."

Back in his bedroom, he undressed, tossed his clothes over a chair and slipped into bed. How could this be happening to him? How could he be losing another woman he loved? He turned his head toward the night stand and stared at the empty space where Harriet's picture had sat for the last eighteen months. He'd removed it only a week ago, hoping to get one of Diana to replace it.

A ball of misery welled up in his chest. Why hadn't she come to him herself? When he thought of all the outrageous things she'd said in the past, he could find no excuse for her behavior. She should have told him how she felt.

He could call her and explain or beg her to understand his failure to tell her he loved her. He could beg her to take her ring back and promise to marry him after all. But she wouldn't unless he said those three little words that stuck in his throat. How could he expect her to understand that he hadn't said them because it hadn't felt right saying them to a woman other than Harriet?

The words *I love You* rolled so easily off her tongue. How could he expect her to understand his inability to say them even though he felt them? How could he convince her he'd loved her for weeks?

He lay on the bed, feeling overwhelmed with grief and sorrow. "Oh, Lord, please help me!" he prayed. Then, without conscious thought, he slipped out of bed, got down on his knees, and prayed.

He prayed until his knees felt numb and words no longer came. Then he continued kneeling before God, letting all the hurt, anger, and pain that had built up in him since Harriet's death flow out.

When it was done, he sprawled out on the floor, too drained and weary to climb back into bed. He felt strangely vitalized. He still didn't know what he was going to do about Diana, but just for that night, he wasn't going to worry about it anymore. He didn't need to. He'd thrown it all on God.

"I know it's unfair and it's short notice, but I have to have a few days off," Diana told Becki the next morning as they had their morning tea.

She didn't look away as Becki studied her face. She was pretty certain it was obvious she'd been crying most of the night, and she knew Becki had noticed that she no longer wore David's ring. "Do you want to talk about it, Di?"

She shook her head. "I know it's cowardly, but I can't face Carolyn just yet. I don't know what to say to her. She'll probably hate me."

"Don't worry. We'll manage. And don't worry about Carolyn, either. Let that idiotic father of hers explain how he screwed up."

"Becki! He's not an idiot!" she protested.

"Any man who's too stupid to tell the women he loves that he does love her is a big-time idiot!"

"Did it ever occur to you that he doesn't love me?"

"No, that didn't occur to me."

"Why not?"

"I saw the way he looked at you when we were all at the carnival."

"Some people would call that passion."

"Well, they'd be wrong," Becki insisted. "I know love when I see it shining in an idiot's eyes."

"Becki!"

Becki slammed her cup down so hard her saucer rattled. "For two cents, I'd call him and give him a—"

"No! Just give me a few days to pull myself together."

Becki nodded, squeezed her shoulder, and let herself out of the apartment.

"You are the biggest nut this side of the milky way!"

David narrowed his gaze and glared across his trailer office at Mike. "Thanks for the support!"

"I'm going to give it to you straight. You're a fool. Harriet is dead. You're alive. You and Carolyn have a right to have a woman in your life that you both love." Mike frowned. "Speaking of Carolyn, how's she taking this?"

"Better than I thought. My mother talked to her before I could. I don't know what she told her, but Carolyn seems to think that things are going to work out. She said she'd prayed for me and Diana."

Mike nodded. "Never saw a man who needed it more. What is so hard about telling her you love her? You just open your mouth and say the words and your world's right side up again."

He shook his head. "It won't be that easy. Maybe it would have been if I'd done that as soon as I found out how she felt, but now she's going to want me groveling at her feet."

Mike shrugged. "So? She wants groveling, give her groveling. Unless you think she's not worth it."

"She's worth it," he said and suddenly knew that she was.

"Then what are you waiting for? Get out of here and go tell her. I'll hold down the fort while you're gone."

David sprang to his feet and bolted for the door. He drove over to his mother's house straight from the site to ask her to keep Carolyn for the weekend.

"I'd be delighted to. Oh, David, I was beginning to think you were going to let her slip through your fingers and she's just so exactly what both you and Carolyn need," she sobbed into his shoulder.

"I know, Mom. I know. I'm going to do my best to make up with Diana, but she might not be interested in me anymore," he said in a bleak voice.

"Nonsense, dear. She'll be delighted to see you." She wiped at her tears and looked anxiously into his face. "Provided you're prepared to tell her what she needs to hear."

He nodded quickly and she smiled and hugged him. "Good. Now go tell Diana you love her."

Armed with a dozen roses, he drove to Diana's apartment. As he waited for her to answer the door, he felt warm and happy at the prospect of seeing her again. He came crashing back down to earth when a man came to the door. "Yeah?"

He stared at the tall, dark man facing him. "Ah...I was looking for Diana."

"She's in the shower."

She was in the shower while this man was in her apartment? Who was he anyway? Less than a week ago she'd been engaged to him, now she was showering with strange men in her apartment?

A surge of jealousy sliced through him. How could she? "Thanks." His stomach churned until it was tied into knots of agony as he hurried across the sidewalk, intent on getting away from there. He had the SUV's door open when the man caught up with him. "Hold on a second."

He turned to glare at the man and shook his head. "We don't have anything to say to each other."

"You're too right, but Di will probably kill me if I don't tell you I'm Hank Stuart."

He was so relieved he actually had to lean back against the SUV and closed his eyes briefly. "Her...?"

He shot a cool look David's way. "Her cousin. Who did you think I was? Her boyfriend?"

Shame that he had thought that of Diana kept him silent.

"You must be the guy she's been breaking her heart over."

David sighed. "I'm here hoping to make that up to her."

"Hurt her again and you'll have to answer to me," Hank Stuart promised in a low, no-nonsense voice.

David nodded too relieved to be annoyed. "Understood."

He gave David another long, cool look. "You'd better come upstairs. I don't know why, but I think she might actually want to see you."

Chapter Seventeen

David's heart beat like an out of control jack hammer as he followed Hank Stuart up the two flights of stairs. Once inside the apartment, Hank picked up his jacket and headed for the door.

He turned to face David. "The next time I see Diana, I hope she won't have tears in her eyes. Unless they're happy ones."

When he was alone in the living room, David paced back and forth in front of the window, practicing what he would say to Diana. But when she finally came into the living room half an hour later, he stared silently at her.

"David!" For a moment her beautiful gaze lit up and she smiled, then she fled back into the bedroom. He heard the door slam with a sinking heart.

He waited for fifteen minutes before he realized she had no intentions of returning to the living room. He walked down the hall and tapped on the only closed door, which he decided must be her bedroom.

"Diana, I need to talk to you."

"Please go away, David."

"I can't. Not until we talk. I'm sorry I hurt you, honey. Please come out and talk to me."

"Why should I?"

He pressed his face against the door panel. "Because I need you more than I can say. Please, Diana. Come out so we can talk."

There was a long pause, then he heard the doorknob turning. Moments later she opened the door. Her brown eyes were wide and filled with tears.

"How did you get in here? Where's Hank?"

"He left after he let me in. He said you'd probably want to see me."

"Well, just maybe he was wrong."

"I hope not, because I want to see you." His hands shook as he gave her the flowers. "I know I should have called, but I was afraid you'd tell me not to come. And I had to come."

"Why?"

It was the moment of truth. Their relationship would either flourish or end on what he said next. "Because I love you."

Her mouth fell open and she stared up at him. "What? What did you say?"

He caressed her cheek. "I love you. I love you. I love you, I love you, and I love you."

Tears spilled down her cheeks. She clutched the roses against her chest. "You...do?"

"Yes, I do. And I'm so sorry that I didn't tell you sooner. It's just that I felt guilty for falling in love with you so soon after Harriet's death."

She pulled away from his caressing hand and leaned back against the bedroom door. "What's changed?"

"Nothing. I just realized that Harriet loved me as much as I loved her. If I had died, I would have wanted her to go on with her life. I know she would have wanted me to fall in love again. I have. With you.

"Please marry me. I will love you as much or more than I loved her and I will never, ever give you cause to doubt my love again."

Tears flowed freely down Diana's cheeks now. She opened her arms. "I need a hug. Would you please hold me?"

"Oh, yes!" Tossing the roses into the bedroom, he wrapped his arms around her. He hugged her tight, burying his face against her neck. "Forgive me for hurting you. I'm so sorry."

For a while she was content to just cry in his arms, but when he put a hand under her chin to lift her face, she welcomed the sweet pressure of his lips on hers. She responded warmly, parting her lips under his. He kissed her breathless.

Feeling her desire heating up, she pulled out of his arms. "Is it getting hot in here or it just me?"

He laughed, caressing her cheek. "It's absolutely not just you."

She sighed. "David, are you sure?"

"About wanting to marry you?"

"About loving me?"

"I'm very sure, Diana. You might like to know that I've removed all the pictures of Harriet from the house and put them in a scrapbook for Carolyn. The only picture left is the one in Carolyn's bedroom."

She watched with anxious eyes as he reached in his pant pocket. Her heart pounded wildly when he held the ring out to her. "Will you marry me?"

This was surely God's will for her. She nodded. "Yes! I will."

He slipped the ring on her finger.

She laughed and threw her arms around his neck. "Oh, David, I love you so much!"

"I love you too, darling."

The look she saw in his eyes was sufficient to remove all her doubts. "Suppose you show me how much you love me?"

He accepted her invitation, drawing her into his arms.

She slid her palms up his chest to link her arms around his neck.

His mouth descended on hers. He kissed her with a passion and fervor that left her feeling weak and longing for more.

With her senses overwhelmed, she lost track of everything except the passion he ignited in her. She made no effort to slow things down between them until she felt his fingers moving against her bodice buttons.

She pushed her hands against his shoulders. "No, David."

He sighed and released her. "Sorry."

"It's all right, but there are limits to how far we can go before we're married."

"I know."

"And you're all right with that?"

"No, but I doubt if that's going to change your boundaries."

"You're right. It's not."

He shrugged. "No harm in trying."

"Nice try." She took his hand and led him back into the living room where they sat together on the love seat.

"How is Carolyn? Is she very angry with me?"

He caressed her cheek. "No. Mom told her to pray for us instead of getting angry or worrying."

"And that worked?"

"Yes, because Mom told her we loved each other, and we would get back together before long, and she believed it. She has missed seeing you, though."

She turned her head and kissed his fingers. "I've missed her, too."

"Is Carolyn the only one you missed?"

"No. Of course not." She sighed. "I'm sorry I was such a coward about everything, David. I should have told you how I felt."

"I should have made it unnecessary for you to feel that way." He kissed her cheek. "I'll do my best to make sure it doesn't happen again."

She smiled. "Yeah. You see that it doesn't." She felt his chest shake with laughter and turned to look at him. "What's so amusing, buster?"

He shook his head. "Just thinking what an idiot I've been. I should have known I didn't stand a chance the moment I saw you."

"As I remember, you weren't very impressed the moment you saw me."

"You are so wrong, sweetheart. I told myself I wasn't impressed, but you're a beautiful woman. I couldn't stop thinking about you. I kept telling myself you weren't my type, but deep down inside, I knew you were. My heart knew from the moment you started flirting with me that it was yours for the taking. It just took the rest of me awhile to face the truth."

"Which is?"

"That I love you to complete and utter distraction."

She smiled and turned back in his arms, snuggling against his chest. "God is good," she said softly.

His arms tightened. "Yes," he echoed. "He is. He sent you to me just when I needed you most to heal my heart and help me regain my faith."

She twisted around in his arms to look at him again. "Your faith, David? Then you've reconciled with God?"

He nodded. "Yes. And I know I don't have to tell you how it feels. The last eighteen months have been the worst in my life.

Mostly because I didn't rely on the Lord's love and ability to heal all the hurts and pains in life like I should have. I made it worse than it needed to be for me and Carolyn. God sent you to us to make it better."

He sighed. "It took falling in love with you to make me realize how good the Lord is. I lost Harriet and I never thought I'd be happy again. But I am with you. Carolyn and I both love you."

She leaned up and kissed his cheek. "And I love you both. Oh, David! I can't tell you how happy it makes me to hear you talk about God with love."

"I'm happy, you're happy. But you can make me happier than I am now," he told her.

"Y'all just name the way and I'm right on it," she teased.

"By setting a date for this big, formal, but hopefully not-too-far-in-the-future wedding of ours. When will you marry me, my darling?"

"I've had time to think David, and if you're really set against it, we don't have to have a formal wedding. We could get married quietly as soon as possible. We—"

"No. I want our wedding day to be everything you want and expect it to be. It might kill me, but I'll wait."

She lifted his ringless left hand and kissed the third finger. "I haven't been entirely fair."

"Yes, you have."

"No. I really haven't. I've been thinking that I wouldn't mind if you wore the ring Harriet gave you on your right hand."

He sat back against the love seat and turned her all the way around to face him. She saw the look of surprise on his face. "Diana?"

"No. I mean it. I know it meant a lot to you because she gave it to you. You shouldn't have to keep it hidden away." She took a deep breath. "And we can put some of her pictures back. She was Carolyn's mother and the love of your life."

"Yes, she was. Now you are."

"I know," she said with satisfaction. "And I don't need to be jealous of the woman who gave you and Carolyn everything you needed. You both have a right to your happy memories of her without worrying that I'll be jealous. I just hope that with the Lord's help, I can do as well for you as she did. We'll make our own memories to add to the other happy ones you two already have."

He shook his head, an amazed look on his face. "You are an incredible woman."

She grinned up at him. "I'm glad you finally realize that."

"I do and I love you, Diana Stuart."

"Of course you do," she said, filled with an incredible sense of contentment. "And just in case you should forget in the future, I'll be sure to remind you to tell me on a regular basis. Say for breakfast, lunch, and dinner." She shrugged. "Maybe at snack time, too."

He laughed, and cupping her face in his hands, he kissed her. It was a sweet, tender kiss that held all the promise of love and happiness she'd ever wanted or expected out of life.

Then they knelt on the floor together and said a prayer of thanksgiving for all God in his goodness had provided.

The End

Meet Marilyn Lee

Plus you can visit her website to find out more about her and her coming soon books as well:

http://www.marilynlee.org

To subscribe to Marilyn Lee's Love Bytes,

marilynlee-subscribe@yahoogroups.com

After her bio you will see her books listed that she has out. Many of her books are both in ebook and print formats.

Marilyn lives, works, and writes on the East Coast of The US. In additional to thoroughly enjoying writing erotic romances in various genres, she enjoys roller-skating, spending time with her large, extended family, and rooting for all her favorite hometown sports teams.

Her other interests include collecting Doc Savage pulp novels from the thirties and forties and collecting Marvel comics from the seventies and eighties (particularly Thor and The Avengers.) Her favorite TV shows are forensic shows, westerns (Gun smoke and Have Gun, Will Travel are particular favorites), and mysteries (Charlie Chan movies in particular).

Her all time favorite mystery movie is probably Dead, Again. She's seen nearly every vampire movie or television show ever made (Forever Knight and Count Yorga, Vampires are favorites. She thoroughly enjoys interacting with readers either through email or via her Yahoo web group.

Red Rose™ Publishing

Summer Storm-ebook and print available

Skin Deep-ebook and print available

Night Heat- ebook available and coming soon to print

Eye of the Beholder- ebook available and coming soon to print

Ellora's Cave

Bloodlust series:

Bloodlust 5-Midnight Shadows
Conquering Mikhel Dumont
Taming Serge Dumont
Forbidden Desires
Nocturnal Heat
All In The Family
The Talisman
Teacher's Pet
Night of Desires
Trina's Afternoon Delight

Branded
Moonlight Desire
Moonlight Whispers
Road To Rapture
The Fall of Troy
Full Bodied Charmer
Breathless In Black
Playing With Fire
White Christmas
Pleasure Quest
Quest III—Return to Volter

Liquid Silver Books

Yesterday Day's Secret Sins

Changeling Press

Moonlight Healing
Soul Mates
Moonlight Madness Books I & II
Daughters of Takira Series:
One Night in Vegas
Kyla's Awakening
Revelations
Daughters of Takira—complete series

Loose id

Falling For Sharde
Nice Girls Do
Dream Lover
The Dare
Fantasy Knights

By Genre
I/R themes or couples

Teacher's Pet
Moonlight Healing
Night of Desire
Soul Mates
Summer Storm
Bloodlust 5-Midnight Shadows
Trina's Afternoon Delight
Taming Serge Dumont
Forbidden Desires
Nocturnal Heat
All In The Family
The Talisman
Moonlight Desire
Moonlight Whispers
Playing With Fire
White Christmas
Pleasure Quest
Quest III—Return to Volter
Primal Lusts
Moonlight Madness Books I & II
Revelations
A Thing Called Love (also available in paperback)
Falling For Sharde
White Christmas
Where You Find It (written as Mary Lynn)

BBW heroines

Teacher's Pet
Trina's Afternoon Delight
Nice Girls Do
The Fall of Troy
Full Bodied Charmer

Playing With Fire
Falling For Sharde
Bloodlust—Nocturnal Heat

Contemporary settings

Teacher's Pet
Night of Desire
Soul Mates
Trina's Afternoon Delight
The Fall of Troy
Full Bodied Charmer
Playing With Fire
Falling For Sharde
White Christmas

Romantic suspense themes

Yesterday's Secret Sins
A Thing Called Love

Paranormal themes

Moonlight Healing
Soul Mates
Fantasy Knights
Bloodlust 5-Midnight Shadows
Conquering Mikhel Dumont
Taming Serge Dumont
Forbidden Desires
Nocturnal Heat
All In The Family
The Talisman
Moonlight Desire
Moonlight Whispers
Road To Rapture

Pleasure Quest
Quest III—Return to Volter
Branded
Primal Lusts
Moonlight Madness Books I & II
Daughters of Takira Series:
One Night in Vegas
Kyla's Awakening
Revelations
Daughters of Takira—complete series

2556256

Made in the USA